Church Girls

By Sheridan S. Davis

Church Girls

Published by Chocolate Chip & Co., LLC
Chicago, Illinois
chocolatechipandco@gmail.com

Cover Design by Charles Reese | Design by Charles
Email: reese.charles@icloud.com

Copyediting by Sitara Thomas and Cheryce Thompson

ISBN: 978-1727208559 | Paperback

Printed in the United States of America

Sheridan S. Davis

Acknowledgements

Firstly, I owe a huge THANK YOU to my Lord and Savior, Jesus Christ! He is literally the head of my life! Thank You, Jesus, for the gift of the scribe and for always loving me! Literally my BEST friend!

I also thank God for my family, which includes my parents: Apostle Joseph and Pastor Trina; siblings: Jamilia, JJ, Shakale, and Jayla; Grandparents; Aunties; Uncles; and cousins. I love you all. I specifically thank Mama, Daddy, Tara, First Lady Natalie, Charles, Cheryce and Jayla for offering your opinions and help during the writing process.

A huge thank you to Keisha Ervin, a Best-Selling author, for your videos, being an example of dopeness, and laughter you provide! Thank you for being my big sis!

Thanks to Dr. Syleecia for her daily words of encouragement! I'm a Visionaire!

I thank my church family, Word for The World Ministries International and my PCHIEF family for every form of support. You guys mean the World to me.

Lastly, to every friendship that inspired this book

Shakale Davis' EP, "Note to Self" and "Superwoman" by Karen White have been the soundtrack to this book.

Sheridan S. Davis
Bobbie Jean Milton, I wrote another book!

Sheridan S. Davis

Sheridan S. Davis

Dedication

This book is dedicated to those I lost in September, especially Granddaddy. I miss them so.

Other Titles by Sheridan S. Davis

"Saved Sex"

"Pretty for A Dark-Skin Girl"

"I'm Nobody's Ruth"

All available on Amazon.com

Table of Contents

Sheridan S. Davis

Chapter 1

*L*ife is good, Shyanne thought to herself as she stood before her mirror untwisting her natural hair. Her fit—but still thick—body was wrapped in her favorite blue, terrycloth bath towel. That thing was old. She'd had it since she was 16 years old, and still, at the age of 25, Shyanne refused to let that holey towel go.

"Wait a minute. That's my song!" Shyanne wiped her Shea Butter covered fingers onto her towel, sashayed over to her computer to turn the volume up, and began singing and rocking her full hips to the beat.

"Your eggs are over easy, your toast done lightly. All that's missing is your morning kiss that used to greet me!" She joined in the middle of the verse, sang and danced in full concert as if she had an audience. "Sing it, Karyn!" She encouraged.

You see, although Shyanne Lawson was only 25 years old, she loved her some dusties. Her radio stayed between Chicago's famous station for throwbacks, V-103, or the gospel station, 1390. She was quite different from her peers. If you pointed a gun to her head and forced her to quote the Migos or even 2 Chains, she couldn't do it; but she could belt out some Whitney, Luther,

1

Aretha, Patti, Kirk, Donnie, Yolanda, or Milton any day of the week.

"I'm not your Superwoman!" She sang with conviction, "I'm not the kind of girl that you can let down and think that everything's ok. Boy, I am only hu-u-u-maaaan!" She inserted a churchy run and gospelized the song. "This girl needs..."

Just as she was about to get her Prince on, her phone rang, bringing her crashing down off her imaginary stage and face-first into reality.

Who is this interrupting me? she thought, as she reluctantly turned Karyn White's "Superwoman" down and checked her phone. Her furrowed brow was immediately put at ease when she saw the name "Darrien Roberts" dancing across her screen. Her size 14 body jumped up and down 3 times; she was excited to hear from him. Shyanne hurriedly answered his call.

"Hello?", she answered, out of breath.

"Hey, my Shy. How are you? Did I catch you at a bad time?" Darrien wondered. He'd noticed her breathlessness and figured she was busy.

"No, you didn't catch me at a bad time. I'm actually getting dressed to go out with the girls tonight." Shyanne looked at the time and noted she was at least 30 minutes behind schedule. *Shoot!* Shyanne was habitually late. She swore to her friends that she'd be on time tonight; but instead of proving them wrong, she'd be validating their claims once again. She had 1/4th of her flat twists to take out and she hadn't even put on her coconut oil, makeup, or clothes. But despite all that, she wasn't missing Darrien's call.

Shyanne wasn't as blessed in the love department as her friends. Heck, her friend Lisa had already lost her virginity by the time they were 18. Shyanne was waiting until marriage and was very proud of that fact. Because of her stance on abstinence, and her overall good-girl, church persona, she didn't have many eligible suitors. She was a beautiful, statuesque girl, standing 5'10" tall. She was curvy in all the right places. She had plenty wagon she was dragging, she wore a 36 C bra, and had solid, thunder thighs. And although she was thick, she had washboard abs and toned, but not too toned, arms. She had pouty, full lips, dimples so deep you could place your fingers inside, and chocolatey skin. Shyanne had long, thick natural hair that, when straightened, landed at her waist.

Shyanne wasn't your typical Instagram "baddie", but she was beautiful. Aesthetically, she would put you in the mind of a dark-skinned version of the late, great singer Phyllis Hyman. Sure, heads turned when Shyanne walked into a room, but she never noticed it. Shyanne never wore clothes to showcase her frame. Her friends often teased her, referring to her as "Mother Shyanne" because she'd rather wear an over-sized top and some designer jeans than a bodycon dress. Shyanne was the epitome of a church girl, not the negative stereotype—she was a good girl.

"I bet you're running late. What time are y'all supposed to go out? It's 6:45 now." Darrien said, catching Shyanne off guard.

Shyanne smiled to herself. "You swear you know me so well. You don't know me, Darrien. I'm getting ready."

"I know you're smiling right now. You probably aren't even dressed."

"What makes you think I'm smiling?" Shyanne quickly pursed her lips together, forcing herself to stop smiling.

"I know you're smiling," he corrected her, "because I know I make you smile, right my Shy?"

"Oh, so you think you got it like that?"

"I know I got you like that."

Shyanne went silent. *Dang, is it that obvious?*

Shyanne knew it was true. She was trying to catch herself because, surely, she was cascading into love with Darrien.

Darrien was the 32-year-old assistant pastor to his father's church. Darrien and Shyanne had so much in common. Both were bishops' children. Shyanne's father, Bishop Steven Lawson, Sr., is the Bishop and founder of the largest church on Chicago's west side, Freedom Temple. He is both loved and criticized by many across the city and even the country. Freedom Temple hosted many major conferences, helped countless homeless people and was a source for many disenfranchised people citywide. Many ministers from Freedom Temple went on to start their own ministries across the nation, including Darrien Roberts, Sr.

With Bishop Lawson's blessings, Pastor Darrien Roberts, Sr., opened Freedom Temple – Carbondale, which was in the city of Carbondale, IL, in 2000.

Shyanne and Darrien were distant acquaintances throughout their childhood, before Pastor Roberts planted the church in Carbondale.

Shyanne's father put her in charge of their church's Family and Friend's Day this year. When she was looking for a speaker, her father suggested Darrien, Jr. She'd received his number and called to invite him to speak at the event. For some reason, their personalities were like magnets, involuntarily drawing them to one another. When Shyanne called the man to invite him to speak, she'd gotten her speech down to a science, but when he picked up the phone, all of that went out the window.

"Hello, may I speak to Assistant Pastor Roberts?"

"This is he. May I ask who's calling?"

"*Oh, I thought I was calling an assistant's phone number. I didn't expect to get you directly.*" Shyanne giggled nervously. "*This is Shyanne Lawson, Bishop Steve Lawson's daughter. How are you, sir?*"

"*Sir?*" Darrien said, taken aback. "*Why are you being so formal like you don't know me?*" He laughed.

"*Because I don't know you like that. Besides, this is not a leisure call; this is for ministry.*" She was trying her best to stay professional.

"*Well, Ms. Lawson, what can I do for you?*"

"*Well, Freedom Temple is having a Family and Friend's Day service—*"

"*When is it?*" Darrien cut her off. He was eager to be a part. He would clear his schedule if need be. Darrien greatly admired Bishop Lawson since he was a child. It was an added bonus that he'd get to be in the presence of the beautiful Shyanne.

"*Well, you have four months to prepare. It's not until Sunday, April 8th, in the year of our Lord, 2018.*"

Darrien giggled, "*Shyanne, are you always this churchy?*"

"*Don't laugh at me, Mister Assistant Pastor. We are talking about church business.*"

"*Well, tell Bishop Lawson I'm coming. Now, that that's settled. Are you always that churchy?*"

"*Um...*" Shyanne had only prepared to discuss church business. "*I guess.*"

"*Well, I like that. You seem cool, like not tainted.*"

"Not tainted?"

"Yeah. I can tell you're a real-life good girl. You'd probably make a great First Lady someday."

"Nah, bruh." Shyanne laughed at his observation. *"I'm good with just being a Bishop's daughter. I'm not going to turn around and marry one."* Shyanne thought the idea was absurd, but she'd gotten that her whole life. *"But anyway, thank you for agreeing to be the speaker for the service, I'll let my Dad know. And I'll call you in the upcoming months with the theme. Have a blessed day, Pastor Roberts."*

"Thank you for inviting me. Please, tell my future father in law—I mean Bishop Roberts, I'm elated to come."

"Wait, what?" Shyanne was taken off guard.

"What's your favorite color?"

"Why?"

"Because I want to know."

Shyanne hesitated. This was supposed to be a quick conversation about church, not a personal call about a bunch of nothing. Shyanne didn't like getting to know new people, nor did she have a flair for wasting time. But something was telling her that this wasn't going to be a waste of time.

"Blue."

That was 3 months ago. Shyanne and Darrien ended up speaking for 4 hours that evening and had spoken on the phone every day since then.

"Yeah, alright." She said, not having a witty comeback. "I'm going to put you on speaker phone, so I can finish my hair."

"See, I knew it."

They both laughed.

"What do you guys have planned tonight?" Darrien asked, in an effort to prolong the conversation.

"Oh, nothing much. We're going to see Black Panther and going out to eat."

"Dang, I kinda wanted to see that with you," Darrien said, sounding disappointed.

"Like, a date?" Shyanne asked.

"Yeah. I mean, that's what people do when they like each other, right?"

"Well, yeah; but you never asked me on a date. When do you plan to come back to Chicago to take me on said date? You do know Black Panther's not going to be in theaters when you come for Family and Friend's Day, right?"

"Yeah, smarty pants. I know." Darrien let out a deep, throaty laugh. "I was thinking we could make it happen sooner."

"Oh yeah?"

"Yeah."

"Well, you plan it all out, and we'll see what happens."

"So, for clarity, *The* Ms. Shyanne Janell Roberts is letting me take her on a date?"

"Don't make me change my mind, Darrien Tyler Roberts, The Second. And my name is Shyanne Janell Laaaawsoooon. Make sure it's a good, memorable date and totally worth my time. Ok? I like opulence."

"I know my Shy. You're probably going to have a whole extravaganza planned for our wedding."

"Here you go with this marriage stuff again," Shyanne said, while laughing. "I have to see if you're crazy first."

"You know the deal, Shy."

"Yeah, yeah, yeah. Well, let me get off this phone. I need to put on my clothes and head out. Will you be up late tonight?" Shyanne asked.

"I'm not going to sleep until I know you've made it in. Call me when you get home, my Shy. Don't forget."

"Ok."

Dang, he is something else.

Chapter 2

I t's about time this hussy walked through the door!" Kyra, Shyanne's best friend, exclaimed as Shyanne walked up to their table at Claim Jumper. Shyanne looked especially cute, donning a white, oversized Jibri online tunic, Torrid skinny jeans, leopard Christian Louboutin's, and African print bangles on her right wrist. Her afro bounced and flowed in the Chicago winds as she walked through the door. Her makeup was understated, but beat nevertheless, even down to her soft, pale pink lip gloss. She received compliments on her Afrocentric look as she walked in Claim Jumper, a nice, family-style restaurant and bar located in Oak Brook, a Chicagoland suburb.

"Yes, I ordered my food because I was tired of waiting for you." Lisa chimed in, chomping on fried zucchini.

"I'm sorry, girls. I really tried." Shyanne stuck out her bottom lip, giving her best pouty-faced look.

"Yeah, right," Miriam said, not believing a word that came out of Shyanne's mouth.

All the girls turned their heads, refusing to look at or acknowledge Shyanne's fake, sad face. She was sure to do it again.

"Ugh," Selena, Shyanne's sister, grunted. "I'm tired of you, she said, as she got up and greeted her sister with a one-armed hug.

"I know, Sissy," Shyanne said, forcing her sister to hug her full-on. "I'm going to get better – Girl Scout's Honor," Shyanne said, as she jokingly created a "W" with her fingers, referring to the "Westside."

"You stupid!" Selena, Kyra, Lisa, and Miriam said in unison.

They were an awesome five-some. They all grew up together in church. Selena and Shyanne were blood sisters. They were only 11 months apart, making them Irish twins. They were two of four children born to Bishop Steven and Lady Eva Lawson. The other two were Steven, Jr., and Skylar, who were eighteen and fifteen, respectively. Although Mama Eva and Shyanne loved each other, they bumped heads constantly.

Lisa knew the Lawson family her whole life. Her father was also a pastor and a pillar in the city of Chicago, until his untimely death in 2003. She considered the Lawsons to be like her second family.

Lisa, Selena, and Shyanne met Miriam and Kyra in elementary school and added them to their crew. Kyra instantly became Shyanne's best friend. They were all besties; but Kyra was her ace, her BFF, her chummy. They were inseparable.

As they all sat at the table laughing and talking, Shyanne's phone began to vibrate.

Darrien Roberts:
Hey beautiful. Did you make it to the restaurant safely?

He just called me beautiful, she thought to herself. Shyanne was so giddy over the smallest gestures.

Shyanne:
Hey, love. I'm here with the girls now. Thanks for checking on me. That was sweet. ☺

Darrien Roberts:
Of course. I gotta make sure my bride is safe.

"Shy! Shy!" Selena tried to get her sister's attention. "Earth to Shyanne." She snapped her middle and thumb fingers in Shyanne's face to get her attention.

"What's up?" Shyanne said, as she finally looked up from her phone. She'd read Darrien's text message three times and didn't know how to respond. He would not let up with this marriage talk. It was almost creepy—but she secretly loved it.

"Who is he?" Kyra asked.

"Oop." Said Miriam.

"Who is whom, Kyra?" Shyanne asked, while simultaneously cutting her eyes at Miriam.

"Who is the negro that's got you looking down into your phone and smiling like an idiot?"

"Wait. I was smiling?"

"Um, sus, cheesing. Who is it?" Lisa chimed in.

"Fine." Shyanne sighed. She hadn't told them about Darrien yet because she didn't think there was anything to tell. She'd been in the predicament where she thought the "talking phase" would result in being in a relationship, but things never went beyond that point. She was tired of getting excited and being full of anticipation only to be let down in the end.

"Y'all remember Bishop Darrien Roberts? He's the Pastor of Freedom Temple in Carbondale."

"Girl, I know you ain't messing with the Bishop! His wife is going to kick your young behind." Miriam said.

"Um, no. Settle down, Sheree Whitfield, Jr," Shyanne lectured, referring to Miriam's need to create a storyline, drawing a parallel between her and her favorite reality show, The Real Housewives of Atlanta. "I'm not a harlot like you." Shyanne joked.

"Burn!" Selena egged on her sister.

14

"Quit playing with me, dusty!" Miriam quipped.

"I'm kidding, friend," Shyanne responded. "I'm talking to his son, Darrien, Jr."

"OMG! I am so excited for you, friend! Darrien is a fine piece of chocolate meat AND he's got a coin!" Lisa said, offering her hand to Shyanne for a high-five.

"You are such a gold digger." Shyanne giggled, slapping five with her friend.

"You pronounced that wrong. It's g-o-a-l digger. I've got goals, Ms. Lawson. I can't meet them attracting the spirit of 'broke' into my life."

"Amen!" Kyra chimed in.

"Why do I hang with y'all?" Shyanne jokingly asked. "And Kyra, how are you amen-ing?"

"Because wisdom is wisdom. Cole is a lot of things, but broke is not one of them." She paused. "Now, I did not, nor do I think you should marry for money, but I do know that it's a little easier to feel the love when you don't have to worry about if the gas is going to be cut off tomorrow. I saw enough with my parents. I know no marriage is perfect; but if I can avoid financial problems with my man, I will."

Kyra was the only married girl in the crew. She was 25 years old and married to a pastor. Never did she ever think she would marry a pastor. She saw the things her parents went through in ministry and didn't want to go down that same road. Although her father wasn't a pastor, her mother was a minister. She was strict, and holiness was her favorite subject. For years, her father didn't attend church; but her mother dragged her and her sister, Leah, to church every week all the way in Hammond, Indiana.

Although there was no physical infidelity on her mother's end of the relationship, Kyra did feel as though her mother cheated on her dad with the church. Kyra's dad, John, was just a regular guy. He loved God, but he didn't like congregating with a bunch of strangers every week. John felt like his walk with God was personal, and not to be put on display for public comments.

When Kyra's parents first met, neither of them were churchgoers. But one day, Lisa invited all the girls and their parents to church for a concert, and when the choir started singing "Change" by Tremaine Hawkins, Kyra's mom, Gina, lost it! She began crying, leaping, jumping and asking God to come into her heart for real. She loved God, but she was never concerned with living a saved lifestyle. That day, she was filled with the Holy Spirit. Her daughters and their friends laughed at her display of "catching the Holy Ghost," but Gina didn't care. From then on, Gina lived for Christ.

That was the beginning of the end of John and Gina's marriage. They were officially unequally yoked. Although she wanted her husband to go to church with her, or at least respect her lifestyle change, he refused. She gave God and the church her all – all of her time, energy and effort. She believed God for her husband, but she didn't put the work into her marriage, making her husband feel neglected and left out. John loved his wife, but he felt second, not just to God, but to the church. He didn't feel needed. Gina, Kyra, and Leah were their own church-going family, and he was an outsider. They went just about every day, while he was left home to his own thoughts and needs.

One day, Gina and the girls walked into the door to find John in tears, packing his bags. Kyra was devastated, and never really got over it.

After her parents' divorce, Kyra's family had to downsize their living space. It was very difficult to move forward. When John was in the home, they never wanted for anything. After he left, things were very tight. There were no more luxury vacations. And she had to plan activities with her friends weeks in advance to make sure she had the funds to participate.

She eventually confided in Shyanne, telling her about her family's difficulties. Shyanne never told a soul. She eventually encouraged her mother to allow Kyra to come on family vacations with them. They were like sisters.

Shyanne was shocked when Kyra met and fell in love with a pastor, knowing how she felt the ministry ruined her life as a child. But like the older saints sang, "you can't hide from God, you can't hide."

"I hear you, friend," Shyanne said, as she rubbed her best friend's back.

"So, Shy, how long have you guys been talking? Do you like him? You must like him because you were all on your phone smiling and stuff. What's going on, girl?" Lisa asked, all in one breath.

"Well, dang, girl. You nosey." Shyanne giggled. "To be honest, we've been talking on the phone for about 3 months."

"What?"

"Before you kill me, I didn't say anything because it always starts and ends with 'talking', and I'm tired of making announcements if nothing is going to come of this thing."

"I feel you on that, Shy Shy." Miriam agreed.

"So, y'all have been talking on the phone? He hasn't come up here from Carbondale to see you?" Selena quizzed.

"I was about to ask the same question," Kyra said, with her right brow up, anticipating the answer.

"No." Shyanne hung her head. "This is why I haven't said anything. He says he's into me, but I don't see the effort. We'll see."

"Girl," Kyra emphasized, while taking a sip of her drink.

"And this is why I didn't say anything."

"Well, girl, have you told him you're feeling him, Shy?" Lisa said, "I know how you are. You'll treat a man like he's one of us, then be surprised when y'all end up being like brother and sister."

"That is true though," said Miriam.

"Mmm hmm." Selena and Kyra chimed in in agreement.

"Well, thank you to the Iyanla Vanzant wannabe crew for trying to analyze me and fix my life." Shyanne created air quotes with her fingers, exaggerating the word 'trying'. "But what God has for me is for me. And that's just all you need to know. Now, where is the waiter so we can pay for this dang food and head to the show?"

She knew the girls were right. She did have a hard time creating these bonds with men. She did think Darrien should put in more of an effort to pursue her. *Maybe I'm too available. Hmm...* It was official. Shyanne was going to put Darrien on a wild goose chase.

Sheridan S. Davis

Chapter 3

♛

By the time Shyanne got back home from seeing the late showing of Black Panther with her girls, it was after one o'clock in the morning. She was dog tired. She looked down at her phone, wondering if she should let Darrien know that she made it home and quickly decided against it.

"He's going to have to put in some effort to let me know how he feels," she said to herself, aloud, as she stretched out on her living room's plush couch, fully clothed.

Shyanne was worn out. She owned her own plus size boutique, "Pizazz," in the West Loop. It was lucrative – so lucrative, in fact, that she was able to purchase her own 2-unit, 2 story duplex in Chicago's West Town neighborhood, for her 25th birthday last June. She lived in one of the units and rented the other out.

Shyanne loved her place. Her style was Afrocentric, but glamorous at the same time. Her living room was adorned with gray, gold, white, and blush details. Her father purchased a big, gray sectional sofa for her living room. She decorated the couch with white faux fur, gold sequins, and blush throw pillows. She had shiny, hardwood floors with a large white, faux fur resting on top of it. Shyanne loved to rub her freshly pedicured feet on that rug. On top of that plush rug lies a beautiful, marble and gold coffee table. She had Ebony and Essence magazines, and a floral arrangement decorating her table. Above her sofa, she had a huge, gold acrylic wall clock, which was the statement piece of the room. She loved to find beautiful pieces that didn't cost much money.

Facing her sofa was a flat screen television that was mounted on the wall. Underneath was a marble bookshelf with gold accents, housing plenty of books, including her Bible, photos of her family, African masks, and different knick-knacks she'd acquired. Adjacent to her sofa were beautiful bay windows. Shy loved to just look out the windows and dream.

As soon as she laid her head down on the couch, her phone vibrated, startling her out of her sleepy trance. The name *Darrien Roberts* danced across her screen. She immediately swiped left to ignore the call. Shyanne was serious about making him earn her time. She put her phone on Do Not Disturb and surfed the channels on her television screen.

When she didn't find anything on television, she decided to get her sleepy self off the couch, take a shower, and go to bed. Her hair just wasn't going to get twisted up tonight. She was too tired, and she had church all day tomorrow.

Freedom Temple had three services every single Sunday; and because she was a leader in the ministry, she had to attend all of them. 10 a.m. services were usually filled with the older crowd. Then, there were the 12:30 p.m. services, which brought in the most people. Lastly, every Sunday evening at 7 p.m. their church did a radio broadcast. Broadcast showcased some of Chicago's hottest choirs and preachers. People came from all sides of town, and even the suburbs, to attend the praise party that was sure to ensue at Freedom Temple. Anybody traveling down Roosevelt Road was sure to hear the sounds of praise resonating from the church.

When Shyanne finally got in the bed, it was almost three a.m. She put her phone on her charger and went straight to sleep in her king-sized bed.

Three and a half hours later, Shyanne's eyes popped open to the sound of her alarm. She turned off her alarm. Although she was still sleepy and desperately desired to hit the "snooze" button, she decided to get up and get ready for church.

She knelt on the royal blue, carpeted floors in her bedroom and began to pray.

"Father, thank you for waking me up this morning. Thank You for life, health, and strength. Thank You for my church and biological families. Thank You for my friends. Thank You for calling me Your own. I am submitted to Your will, for it is what's best for me. Please, forgive me for every sin and shortcoming. Forgive me for all my doubts. Help my unbelief. Use me for Your glory. Make me Your miracle. I trust You. In Jesus' name, amen."

Shyanne got up and pulled her clothes for today's services out of the closet. Since it was March and cold, she decided to wear a darker color. "Um...let's go with burgundy."

Shyanne pulled out a burgundy, skater skirt made of scuba material. It stopped right above her knee. She decided to wear a long-sleeved, bubblegum pink bodysuit with it. The beautiful top was a turtleneck with lace details. She loved it, but felt the outfit needed an extra boost. She went in her closet and pulled out a gold, high waist belt, burgundy clutch, and gold rings, all of which she got from her mentor, Camesha, the owner of Pursenalities Boutique, in suburban Oak Park, Illinois.

After she set her clothes out, she turned on some worship music and headed into the bathroom to shower and get ready. She had a feeling that today was going to be a great day.

As she showered, Chicago's own Thompson Community Singers' song, "In My Name", blared from her Bluetooth speaker.

"Just ask. Just ask in My name," Shyanne sang along to the ballad. As the water cascaded down her frame, she began to think.

"Ok, God. I'm going to ask. Can you let me know whether I should give my time to Darrien? Because I don't want to do any more emotional roller coasters. Thanks, Big God."

Once Shyanne got out of the shower, and put on her undergarments, she decided to style her hair in a messy bun at the top of her head. She put on her Berkshire stockings, her clothes and jewelry, then debated what kind of shoes she should wear. She decided to go with a leather nude, pointy pump she got from Nordstrom a few years earlier.

Shyanne grabbed her phone from off the charger and checked her notifications. She had several missed calls and messages from Darrien asking if she made it home safely. She ignored the messages and tossed her phone in her clutch handbag.

Once she'd done her makeup and was pleased with her look, she grabbed her waist length, burgundy fur coat and headed out the door.

When Shyanne pulled up at the church in her white, 2014 Mercedes-Benz C300 Sports car, it was 8:55 a.m.

"Yes!" Shyanne exclaimed, happy she finally made it somewhere on time. She walked into the church and headed straight for her Daddy's office.

"Good morning, Sis. Shyanne," Missionary Tolliver greeted and hugged Shyanne with much enthusiasm.

"Good morning, Missionary." Shyanne hugged back. "Is my Daddy in his office?

"Yes, he is. Just knock on the door. He's in there with today's speaker."

"Ok."

Knock. Knock. Knock.

"Who is it?" Bishop Lawson asked.

"It's me!"

"Come on in, me!"

"Hey, Daddy. Hey, Pastor Thomas." Shyanne said, upon entering her dad's huge office. She took off her coat and delicately placed it on the coat rack.

"Good morning, young lady." Pastor Thomas extended his hand for a handshake that lingered on about two seconds too long. Shyanne snatched her hand away when she felt Pastor Thomas's thumb caressing the back of her hand. *Eww!* He had to be at least 40 years her senior.

"Daddy, I was just coming in to give you a hug before I go up to the choir stand."

"Well, make it a big ole hug, Big Girl." Bishop Lawson said. He and Shyanne had a great relationship. Although Selena was the oldest, Shyanne was the most responsible.

She was his right hand. Shyanne was a miracle baby. She was a preemie, born at 6 months. Bishop and Lady Lawson were at the hospital every day while their second child was in the NICU. Bishop had the responsibility of taking care of both his wife and his daughter. Although it was tiresome, he did it with pride. He loved his family.

Bishop named her Shyanne because every time they had an ultrasound done, the baby had her hands in front of her face. He would say, "That's my shy baby." Eventually, he began calling her "Shy". And when she was born, "Shyanne".

He blamed himself for the breakdown in Shyanne and his wife, Eva's, relationship. They loved each other, but often bumped heads. He figured it was because he shielded Shyanne from the world—that world included Eva.

After she had Shy, she went through a serious bout of postpartum depression. Being the mother of an arm baby and a premature baby, on top of taking care of her duties as a wife and First Lady, proved to be a bit much for her. She could not help but blame herself. She wondered what she'd done to cause Shyanne to be born early. Why couldn't she house a baby full term? What was wrong with her? Their first child resulted in a miscarriage, Selena was born two months early, and now Shyanne. She thought her womb was cursed. Although Shyanne thought her mother resented her and she didn't understand why, the fact is that Eva resented herself.

That resentment Shyanne felt from her mom was the real reason why she saved her money to purchase her own home. Shyanne saved that money from the time she was 16 years old, working at her first job at the DuSable Museum. Shy had always been a go-getter. Her parents taught her how to live on a budget. 10% of her earnings went towards her tithes. And 40% was for her to purchase whatever she wanted because, at that age, she had no rent or bills. The other 50% was put in a savings account. In one year, she had saved almost $14,000. At eighteen, with an investment from her parents, she opened Pizazz. By her 25th birthday, she had saved more than enough money to put a 20% down payment on the $900,000 duplex she now owned. She worked for it. Her dad couldn't have been prouder. That's why at her signing, he told her he would cut the check for her living room and master bedroom furniture.

"Love you, Daddy." She said, as they embraced.

"I love you too. See you inside, "as Shyanne opened the door.

"Oh, and Shy."

"Yes?"

"You look pretty today."

"Yes, she does." Pastor Thomas chimed in.

Shyanne cut her eyes at the older man. "Thanks, Dad."

"And I need you to MC broadcast tonight."

"Really, Daddy? Why can't Lena do it?" Her Dad was always trying to make her speak, or sing, or lead in front of the people. Shyanne didn't want to be the 2nd coming of her father. She just wanted to be normal.

"Yes, really. I need you." He knew saying he needed Shyanne would get her hook, line, and sinker.

"Ugh. Ok. I'll do it." Shyanne pouted, and left the room. She was about to line up with the choir until she saw her Dad's armor bearer, Brother Paul.

"Hey, Brother Paul."

"Hey, Shy."

"Aye, go in there with my Dad. I don't like that man that's in there with him. He looks real shifty." Shyanne whispered in his ear.

She was very protective of her family. For that man to caress her hand in front of her father, and comment on her looks as if he wasn't sitting right there, sent a million red flags up in her mind. The man was disrespectful, and he looked flashy.

"Go take care of my dad."

29

"On it." Brother Paul said and went to the Bishop's office. He knew not to play with Shyanne about her father.

Chapter 4

The first two services were awesome at Freedom Temple. Shyanne and her family went back to her family's house. Her mom, Eva, had prepared a grand spread for Sunday dinner.

"Mom, do you have a big t-shirt or something I could put on? I don't want to get any food or anything on my clothes." Shyanne stood in the doorway of the kitchen and asked.

"Shyanne, you knew you were coming over here. Why wouldn't you bring some clothes to lounge in?" Eva asked. "Never mind. Just go in my big dresser second drawer to the left."

Eva's snappy answer annoyed Shyanne.

"All she had to say was yes or no," Shyanne mumbled to herself as she walked into her parents' master bedroom.

The bedroom was huge. Shyanne looked at the photos in the room. Her mind went on a trip down memory lane. She remembered when they lived in the Austin community. All 6 of them were in a 2-bedroom apartment. Their beginnings were humble.

Bishop ran the church out of their living room. No one had much money—all they had was Jesus and joy. Bishop worked as a teacher at an after-school program on the weekdays. Eva was a stay-at-home mom. Money was tight, but they made due.

One day, Bishop Lawson met a real estate agent named Joy. She put the Lawson family on a six-month plan and helped them to purchase their first home. It was a small, three-bedroom home in Broadview, IL. They loved it.

Eventually, the Lawsons wanted in on the real estate business and began flipping houses. It was extremely lucrative for them. The more people Bishop Lawson met through his career, the more people he invited to church. Eventually, both the church and the home had grown. Bishop Lawson made a promise to God that he would never neglect His house or his house, and he never did.

The church went from not being able to pay for the first family's health insurance to being the largest church on the west side, owning real estate, building a homeless shelter, employing 40 staff members, and having a GED program. It took 30 years, but Bishop was seeing the fruits of his and God's labor.

Shyanne stared at the pictures, and a single tear ran down her right cheek. She was so grateful.

"What are you in here doing?" Lil Steve startled Shyanne and tickled her side.

"Stop it, boy!" Shyanne said erupting in laughter. "I'm about to change in here so get out!"

"So, get out!" Steven mocked Shyanne.

"You are so irritating."

"You are so irritating."

"I am an idiot!"

"I am an idiot!"

"Ha! I got you!" Shyanne said, sticking her tongue out at her brother.

"You're so lame. I'ma leave out so you can change. You look very ugly today, by the way."

"Bye, hater!" Shyanne waved goodbye.

She perused through her mother's drawer and grabbed some Adidas joggers and a white t-shirt, disrobed, and dressed. Although the joggers were a little snug, she still looked cute in the outfit.

Shyanne grabbed her phone and charger from her purse and was about to plug it up when she noticed a few text message alerts from Kyra, Lisa, and Darrien.

Sheridan S. Davis

Kyra:
Sooooooooo...how late did you stay up talking to your "man" last night? Cause I know you ended up folding! LOL! Cole and I are coming to broadcast tonight, BTW! Love you, friend! ♥

Lisa:
Did you talk to ole boy? Lol. Love you, Shy!

Darrien:
Are you just not going to answer my calls and texts? I know you made it in because I saw you on your church's live stream. What's good? Did I offend you?

Darrien:
Call me.

Shyanne responded to Kyra and Lisa and told them to leave her alone. She left Darrien's message alone. She'd probably talk to him tomorrow, but she meant what she said. He needed to show her. He hadn't done that yet. And no, she didn't feel like she needed to tell him how she felt. He needed to just do it.

She put her phone on the charger in her parents' room and joined the rest of the family in the dining room.

"Look who's ready for dinner," Eva said, referring to Shyanne.

Eva was a 50-year-old woman who had aged like fine wine. When she and Shyanne were out, they were often asked if they were sisters. Eva was a brown-skinned woman who stood 5

35

feet and 9 inches tall. She was a slender, yet shapely lady, wearing a size 8. She kept her hair in a short pixie cut and loved to dress up. Although her countenance was stern, she really did have a big heart and a megawatt smile. Shyanne definitely got her dimples from her mom.

"Sorry, y'all. I had to find something that I could fit." Shyanne said, joining her family at the dinner table.

"Yes, chile. You know she had to squeeze all that rump in those pants. I'm sure that took some time," Selena said jokingly.

"That's too much booty in them pants." Their sister, Skylar, sang.

Selena, Skylar, Steven, Jr., and Eva laughed.

"Your mama." Shyanne mouthed to her siblings.

"Ooooooh!" Steven, Jr., instigated.

"Ok, ok, everybody. Let's settle down. Eva, baby would you mind praying over the food?" Bishop Lawson asked.

"Not at all. Let's bow our heads." Mama Eva requested. "Father, we thank You. You have provided for us. You have been faithful to us. You have been there for us. We thank You for this spread that You have provided for us. There are some people in this world who don't know where their next meal is coming from. We are blessed. Please, help us to be a blessing to those who are in need. And we ask You to bless and sanctify this food for the nourishment of our bodies in Jesus' name, amen."

"Amen," the family responded in unison.

"And don't let us get sick or fat in Jesus' name, amen," Shyanne added.

"Girl, hush," Eva said.

Everyone laughed and began to dig in. They talked about their days, church, and everything else. Shyanne was happy to be back to her parents' house and among family, but truth be told, her mind was on Darrien. She was wondering if shutting him out was the right move. She wanted to call him, but she was afraid. She was afraid that if she gave in to him, she'd be in a one-sided love affair. The truth was, her heart already went pitter patter at the sound of his voice. But she needed some concrete evidence that she wasn't in this by herself. It had only been three months, too early for her to start feeling things. So, she'd just back away now while she had the chance.

Chapter 5

♛

After eating and getting ready for church, the family headed over to Freedom Temple for service. Selena decided she wanted to ride with Shyanne instead of her parents. She had to ask her about her relationship with Darrien.

"Sis," Selena got Shyanne's attention from the passenger's seat.

"What's up?" Shyanne asked, turning her radio down.

"What's going on with you and D.J.? You seemed like you were really into him last night at dinner. I haven't seen you act like this before."

Shyanne paused and thought about her answer before responding. "I think he likes me, but I don't know he likes me. So, I'm a little scared. I don't want history to repeat itself. You know what I mean?"

"Yeah, I feel you. So, what are you going to do?"

"I don't really know what I'm going to do or what to do," Shyanne admitted. "I just want to slow myself down. To be honest, I am really, really feeling him."

"Aww, man. I didn't know you were this serious about this last night. Well, I hope it all works out." Selena said sincerely, as they pulled up to the church.

"Thanks. Well, let's get up out of this car and head in the church. Daddy's got me MC-ing broadcast tonight, chile." Shyanne said.

"Let Him use you, daughter." Selena encouraged. "That burgundy fur is sharp, by the way. I'm going to need to borrow that."

"Hello, Sis. Lawson and Sis. Lawson. Let me show you all to your seats." Sis. Little, an usher, greeted them.

"Hey, Sis. Little." Both ladies said.

When they walked into the church, Praise & Worship had already begun. The band was blazing, and the church was in a bonified praise party.

The entire church was singing "Hallelujah". Suddenly, a praise break hit the church and all 1,500 people in the building were up on their feet clapping, dancing, and praising. Shyanne was no different. She began to shout to the beat of the music, praising God for his goodness.

At the end of the song, the praise and worship leader signaled for Shyanne to come and take the mic.

"Praise the Lord, everybody!"

The people began to clap.

"Praise the Lord, everybody! Come on, put those hands together and bless Jesus."

The crowd erupted into an applause.

"Now, listen. We came tonight to lift Jesus. Can I get a witness?"

The crowd praised in response.

"First giving honor to God, who is the head of my life. I give honor to my bishop, Bishop Steven A. Lawson, Sr. Clap your hands for my Daddy, y'all. That's my best friend. I also give honor to my First Lady, Eva Lawson and all the ministers. Can we have all of the ministers to stand, please?"

All the ministers stood and were acknowledged.

"We thank God for all of God's children. Now, at this time, we're going to bring up our choir. Come on, put your hands together for the Voices of Freedom."

The choir began to sing a song declaring somehow, they'd make it home to heaven. Once again, a praise hit. When Shyanne got the mic again, she began to exhort.

"I'll get home some day! I may have problems down here, but someday I'm going to make it. No more sickness. No more struggling. No more heartaches. No more disappointments. I'm

41

going to be with my savior. If heaven is your goal...put ...your ...hands..." Her speech began to slow down.

While everyone was excited, Shyanne suddenly felt nervous. At the very back of the church, in the center double doors, she saw four men entering the sanctuary. The 3rd man turned around to assist the 4th man with his coat and hat. The 3rd man then went out the door heading to the Pastor's Study to hang up the coat and hat. The 2nd man stood still waiting on the 4th man, and the 1st man went to search for an usher to get seats for all 4 men.

The 4th man looked to stand about 6 feet and 4 inches from the ground. He was dark-skinned and seemed to be quite muscular. He had a full beard and mustache, and his hair was fresh. He had a nice, Caesar fade haircut and plenty of waves. He was wearing a navy suit and skinny tie from Giorgio Armani. The suit jacket was single breasted with two buttons and notched lapels.

Shyanne couldn't believe her eyes. The man looked like he smelled delicious. She was stunned but she had to continue to exhort.

"Put those hands together. Aren't you glad to know that heaven is on the other side of this?" Shyanne revved back, "Somebody say 'YES!'"

"YES!" The crowd screamed!

"Oh yes!" Shyanne sang!

Meanwhile, the 4th man's eyes never left her. Even when she exhorted, his gaze only grew more intense.

"My God," Shyanne said, and looked in the audience on the front row to her right. She and Selena immediately locked eyes. Shyanne then knew she wasn't making up what she thought she saw.

The 4 men were now seated in the pulpit on the stage just feet away from her.

"Amen, now, we're going to be in the hands of our own, Bishop Steven A. Lawson, Sr. Clap your hands for him as he comes," Shyanne announced.

Shyanne walked out of the pulpit and avoided the 4th man's eyes.

As her dad began to speak, Shyanne sat next to her sister, Selena.

"Girl, OMG," Selena whispered to her sister.

"Just shut up. I'm trying to make myself disappear."

"My God. Didn't Shyanne do a good job tonight? I almost licensed her to preach up in here today," Bishop Lawson said jokingly. "Please, be seated. I want to acknowledge our pulpit guests..."

Shyanne didn't care about any other man up there but the tall brother whose eyes she was trying to avoid. *Dang, he's fine. All that chocolate.*

"We bless God for Assistant Pastor Darrien Roberts, Jr., from Freedom Temple – Carbondale. I love this young man. He's like a son to me. Pastor, why don't you come up and have some words to say to the people. Clap your hands for Assistant Pastor Darrien Roberts," Bishop Lawson instructed, as he acknowledged the 4th man.

"You better clap for your man," Selena joked with Shyanne.

"Girl, I am single boots," Shyanne said.

"Thank you, Bishop Lawson. I'm so grateful to be here today. I found out that no matter the situation, Christ is the answer. I didn't come here to preach. I really came up here all the way from Carbondale to check on one of my friends." He locked eyes with Shyanne. "You know when you have love for someone, you can't just talk it, you have to be about it," Darrien declared.

"Oh...my...God," Shyanne said just above a whisper.

Selena said, "Girl, I think you just got the proof you were looking for."

"It's just like God. He so loved the world that He gave. When you love someone, you will give of your time, energy, and efforts. And even your money. Amen?"

The congregants laughed and cheered in agreement.

If Shyanne were light-skinned, she was sure to be beat red. She was excited to see him and nervous because of him. The rest of the service was a blur for Shyanne. She didn't hear anything the guest preacher preached. Between her stealing glances at Darrien and her texting her BFF's group chat, she was pretty preoccupied.

Shyanne:
Um... Are you negros at my church?

Kyra:
Yep! And I definitely saw AAAAAALLLLLL of that carrying on! Haa!

Miriam:
I'm not there! What the heck are ya talking about?

Lisa:
Giiiiiiirl, I'm in the balcony! I need a drink after all this tension and staring going on in this pulpit!

Kyra:
Right?! Girl, luuuuuust and heat! He's still looking at Shy Shy right now!

Miriam:
What'd I miss????

Shyanne:
@Kyra, no he ain't!

Kyra:
A LIE!!!!!!

Lisa:

You're delusional, Doll!

Shyanne:
Whatev.

Miriam:
Helloooooo

Kyra:
Gotta go. Church is ending. We'll all chat tonight!

When church was dismissed, Shyanne tried to make a b-line for the restroom. She just wanted to breathe. But church people wanted to stop her, shake her hand, and encourage her to "stay on the wall" every step she took. She just grinned and thanked them all. As soon as she was about to head to the bathroom, her phone vibrated.

Darrien Roberts:
Now that I know your phone isn't broken...because you've been texting the whole service...please, meet me in your dad's office.

Shyanne:
You tried it. Ok. Give me 5 minutes.

Darrien Roberts:
I'll give you 4.

Shyanne:
Blah.

Shyanne went to the bathroom to calm herself down, then made her way to her father's office.

Knock! Knock! Knock!

"Who is it?" Bishop Lawson asked.

"Me!"

"Come in, Shyanne."

"You did a great job," Bishop said, as she entered the room.

"Thanks, Daddy," she said, as she embraced her father. "Darrien," she nodded to acknowledge his presence.

"Shyanne," Darrien said as he stood to hug her.

Mmm... Shyanne thought. She felt so small in his embrace. They were like a perfect fit. They lingered for a moment, then reluctantly released each other. They hadn't physically seen each other in a year, and even then, it wasn't like this. The energy between the two was changing.

"Bishop Lawson?"

"Yes, son," Bishop answered. He could detect the chemistry between the two. He noticed that lingering hug and even the eye contact during service. *Something is definitely happening between these two,* he thought to himself.

"I wanted to ask you for your permission to take your beautiful daughter on a date, sir," Darrien said, with his eyes glued to Bishop Lawson's.

Bishop Lawson's eyes darted over at Shyanne whose eyes were glued to the side of Darrien's head. From the look on her face, Bishop could tell his daughter was in shock.

"Is that right?"

"Yes, sir."

"Well, son, that's up to Shyanne; but I'll tell you like this, you better not hurt her mentally, physically, or emotionally or you will have to deal with me. My daughter was brought up in holiness. She's a holy young woman of virtue. There's no premarital sex going on here. She lives for God. If you take her out, don't think you're taking her into your house or you're going into hers. Do not pressure her into doing anything she doesn't want to do. If you can handle that and she wants to go with you, you have my blessing," Bishop Lawson said.

Shyanne was stunned. No man had ever asked her father's permission to take her on a date before. And her dad's response? She was embarrassed and felt protected all at the same time.

"Yes, sir, Bishop. I can adhere to all of that. Well, Shyanne, will you do me the honor of letting me take you out tonight?"

"Um…" Shyanne hesitated. "Yes, I'd love to."

As cool as Darrien was, he couldn't hide the excitement he felt inside. He tried to hide his smile but couldn't. "Great. We can leave whenever you're ready."

Chapter 6

✦

Shyanne was amazed. She could not believe she was about to go out with Darrien. She told him she needed a few minutes, then she'd be ready to go. It was 8:45 p.m. She left her office and texted the BFF Chat asking all the ladies to meet her in the women's bathroom near her father's office. 3 minutes later, her girls came filing in.

"What's going on?" Kyra asked, becoming the spokeswoman for the group.

"Listen, Darrien came all the way to Chicago to ask my Daddy if he could take me on a date?"

"WHAT?" All the girls said together, then proceeded to start jumping up and down. They were all so excited for their sister and friend.

"Yes, I am stunned. I'll fill you guys in on what exactly happened later. I have to get out of here because he's waiting on me. But Lisa, will you drive my car back to my house? And Lena will you stay over? Just tell Daddy you're spending the night with me. I'm going to ride with him; so, stay up so you can open the door for me tonight." Shyanne said, handing her sister her keys.

"I got you, sister."

"Ok, y'all. I have to go. See y'all later." She hugged her friends and left the bathroom.

"Relax and have fun," Kyra yelled out after her friend.

"You ready?" Darrien asked, as Shyanne approached the church's front doors.

"I am," Shyanne said with a smile.

As they walked out of the church, Shyanne was introduced to Man #1, Man #2, and Man #3. Man #1's real name was Rashawn. He was Darrien's driver. Man #2 and Man #3 were his armor bearers: Marvin and Tim.

"If you ever need something and can't get in touch with me, contact Marvin. He'll take care of you." Darrien instructed.

"Well, depending on how this lil date goes, I may not need to know that tidbit of information." Shyanne joked.

"You will."

When they approached the stairs, Darrien took her delicate hand in his and guided her down the stairs. That stood out to her. Chivalry.

Rashawn pulled the black Tahoe up to them. Darrien opened the car door for her and lifted her into the back seat of the car with a smile. He went to the trunk to grab something. She couldn't tell what it was. The next thing she knew, Marvin was getting into the passenger seat and Darrien was climbing in the back seat to join her.

"Um...didn't you have another friend?" Shyanne wondered where Tim was.

"Yeah, he's trailing us in his car," Darrien informed her. "Anyway, so about us..."

"What about us?" Shyanne asked as she looked out the car's window. She was still shocked.

"I called you a few times. Why didn't you respond?" Darrien asked, as he took her left hand into his.

Instinctively, Shyanne looked at him, then continued gazing out the window. "I don't know." She said softly. She didn't want to admit to him that she was not talking to him, so she could see if he really liked her. That would sound stupid aloud. Plus, she didn't want to seem insecure.

Darrien didn't want to press the issue. He was with Shyanne now and that's all that mattered.

"Anyway, where are we going?" Shyanne asked, now looking in his direction.

"Out," Darrien said.

"Really, Darrien? Out where?"

"It's a surprise. Now, talk to me. How's the boutique going?"

"It's going pretty well. I'm actually preparing a fashion show on June 8th for my birthday and to showcase our summer clothing." Shyanne said proudly.

"Thanks for letting me know when your birthday is." Darrien chuckled. "You need some more models?" Darrien asked, as he released her hand and started posing in his seat.

Shyanne laughed at his silliness. "Um...unless you're a plus-sized woman underneath that suit, you can't be in the show."

"Whoa! So, you want to find out what's underneath this suit? Relax, girl. We ain't even married yet." Darrien joked.

"Negro, please, I'm not marrying you," Shyanne said, as they got off the expressway.

"That's what your mouth says," Darrien shot back.

"So, we're in Hillside." Shyanne began to look around.

They pulled up in front of Jordan Temple, a church in Hillside, Illinois. "Why are we at church? We could've had a date at my church if that's all you wanted to do. I told you to make it special and you take me to church? Really, Darrien?" She was over the date before it even began.

"Calm down," Darrien said, as he got up out of the car. He walked around the back of his Tahoe and opened Shyanne's car door. He extended his right hand to help her get out of the vehicle.

Shyanne hesitated. She looked around and wondered what he was up to, but she decided to go ahead and go on the date. She grabbed her purse with her left hand and gave Darrien her right. They began to walk down the street. Shyanne hoped they wouldn't be walking long because her nude, pointy toe pumps were not walking shoes.

They crossed the street and were heading in the direction of Priscilla's, a soul food restaurant in Hillside. Shyanne's stomach growled at the sight of the restaurant's signage.

"Is this where we're going? Aren't they closed?" Shyanne inquired.

"You ask too many questions," Darrien said, as he held the door open for her. She walked in, and the restaurant was empty except for one, candlelit table set for 2. Shyanne was stunned.

"Aww, Love! You didn't have to do that." Shyanne turned around and hugged her beau. Now, this was special. Priscilla's closed at 8 pm on Sundays. She didn't know how Darrien got them to stay open later and decorate on top of that. Not to mention, she loved soul food and could not to wait to order.

"This is really sweet," Shyanne said again, as she let him go and gazed into his small brown eyes.

"I'm glad you like it. You wanted special, right?" Darrien asked, pulling out Shyanne's chair for her.

"That's right," Shyanne said, as she took a seat and removed her fur coat.

"Here's special. I called the owner to get them to keep this spot open just for the two of us for dinner. Take a look at your menu and let me know what you want to eat."

"Wow. Well, you don't have to do anything else. I love to eat. So, I'm happy." Shyanne said, as she looked over the menu. "And soul food ain't cheap; so, that's a brownie point for you." She joked.

Darrien laughed as he, too, perused the menu.

"Ok; I think I'm ready. I want the Cornish hens, macaroni and cheese, greens, and candy yams. Skip my diet, it's a celebrate," Shyanne chuckled.

"You don't need a diet anyway. You're perfect as is." Darrien winked. "Mrs. Priscilla, we're ready to order," he called out.

Did he just say I'm perfect? Shyanne thought to herself.

"May I have a veggie plate with mac and cheese, corn, cabbage, and dressing? And this beautiful young lady will have Cornish hens, macaroni and cheese, greens, and candy yams." He ordered for the both of them—he was a complete gentleman. "My Shy, is there something you wanted to drink?" He turned and faced Shyanne.

"Um...I'll take the sweet tea."

"And I'll just have water," Darrien said.

"Coming right up, guys." Mrs. Priscilla, the owner, said.

"So, Darrien, how'd you know I was going to let you take me out tonight? You had this all planned out."

"Truth be told, when you started ignoring me, I figured I had to step my game up. Although we're not together together yet, I still enjoy getting to know you. Not talking to you just wasn't an option for me. So, if it took a 6-hour drive up here to get your attention, that's what I'd do." Darrien confessed.

"Well, you have my attention. What are you going to do with it?" Shyanne asked, as she took a sip of water.

"Utilize it until you see we belong together," Darrien said with a straight face.

"Here you go with these marriage jokes again. Slow down, little red Corvette." She said, quoting Prince.

"I'm not joking though. I'm going to be straight up because that's all I know how to be. I'm not looking for a girlfriend, I'm looking for a wife. I've had girlfriends. I need my rib," he paused. "To be honest, I've been praying that I would find my wife. I'm tired of dating."

"I feel you on that," Shyanne admitted.

"And if I can be more candid," Darrien sat up straight and looked Shyanne directly in her eyes, "You look like her to me."

"I look like who?"

"The one that I prayed for."

"Wow." Shyanne clutched her invisible pearls, "What kind of game are you trying to run on me?" she asked. The revelation that he actually wanted to marry her was mind-blowing. She looked him in the eye to see whether or not he was just running game. The thing is, she wasn't picking up any red flags. Usually, a man confessing this type of thing would make her, or any woman for that matter, feel like he was either crazy or just trying to get in her pants; but she wasn't getting that feeling from Darrien.

"Game? Look, I'm too old to play games. I'm not playing with you. I'm being real. Now, I need you to be real. Are you seeing anybody else?"

"Ok, Pastor, here's you and your lady friend's food," Mrs. Priscilla announced.

"Thank you so much," Darrien smiled.

Dang, he has a cute smile, Shyanne thought to herself. *Get it together, girl. Just have a good time.*

"Wow. Everything looks so good. Thank you," Shyanne agreed, coming out of her shell.

"You're welcome, sweetie. Enjoy." Mrs. Priscilla said, as she left the two of them alone.

"You want to bless the food?" Darrien asked.

"Sure." They held hands and bowed their heads. "Father, we thank you for allowing us to gather together. Thank you for being an all-seeing and all-knowing God. I pray that you would bless this food, the hands who prepared it, and the pockets that are paying for it. And please, don't let us get sick or fat. In Jesus' name, amen."

Shyanne opened her eyes and found Darrien looking at her like she was crazy. Darrien burst out laughing at the last 2 lines of the prayer.

"Hey, King Jesus knows my heart." Shyanne joined in the laughter.

"So, back to my question," Darrien steered the conversation.

"Which was?"

"Are you seeing anybody?"

"First of all, this Cornish hen is bomb. Anyway, no, I'm not seeing anyone." Her eyes connected with Darrien's. "But you should know that because I've spoken to you every day for the last 3 months and 1 week. I couldn't really do that if I had a man," Shyanne said, as she continued eating her food.

"People do it all the time," Darrien said in between chews.

"I'm not people," Shyanne said, looking him dead in the eye. "Don't compare me to them. I'm different."

"I know. That's what I like about you," Darrien revealed.

"Good. Tell me something that most people don't know about you," Shyanne inquired.

"Well, I'm afraid of the dark. I sleep with the television on because I need the light to sleep. That's embarrassing but it's the truth," he shared.

"Are you serious?" Shyanne inquired.

"Yeah," Darrien bowed his head in shame.

"That's crazy because I sleep with the T.V. on, too. I can't relax when it's pitch black. I read somewhere that it's spiritual. Like, different spirits manifest in the dark and people like us have sensitive spirits or something," Shyanne reassured.

"Really? So, what kind of T.V. shows do you like to watch?"

"I hate to admit it but I'm a reality T.V. head. I watch the Love and Hip Hops, Real Housewives of Atlanta and Potomac, and Iyanla. My favorite sitcoms tend to be from the 90's. I love me some Living Single, Martin, and A Different World. Oh, and I used to like Scandal, but they lost me when Olivia got kidnapped that one season. I haven't been able to follow since then," Shyanne stated, as she chewed her food.

Darrien looked at her in amazement. They had so much in common. They'd known each other since childhood but getting to know grown woman Shyanne was so intriguing. Darrien never wanted their conversations to end. He saw forever in her eyes. She wasn't ditsy, overly aggressive, or embarrassing. Shyanne had a flair—she could be cool in the White House or the neighborhood soul food restaurant. She was just cool. Darrien did notice she was hesitant to completely let her wall of protection down, but he prayed that eventually, she would. Little did Darrien know, he had Shyanne hook, line, and sinker.

"Can I ask you a question?" Shyanne asked.

"What's up?" Darrien asked, as he put his fork down and gave her his undivided attention.

"This may sound stupid but what do you want to be when you grow up? Where do you want to be when you grow up? I know you're 32, but you know what I mean." Shyanne was asking sincerely. Ambition was attractive to her. A man could be as fine as wine but if he did not have goals, it was a wrap.

"That's actually a good question. When I grow up, I want to be a homeowner, continue to be a man of God, have a wife and family. I would like to have a film production company as well. And where would I like to be? I'd like to be next to you and our kids."

"Okay! Well, you tried it, but those are some nice goals. I'm actually impressed. You can definitely achieve those, you know? You just have to work on it," Shyanne encouraged, as she rubbed his arm.

"Thank you, Shy," Darrien smiled and asked, "may I ask you a question now? And will you be honest with me?"

"Um...yeah," Shyanne said removing her hand. "What's up?"

"Do you like me?" Darrien asked.

Shyanne turned her head to the side.

"Why can't you look at me?" Darrien asked, as he lovingly took her face in his hands and made her face him. "I'm over here. What's good? Be real."

Shyanne hesitated and then responded with a throaty, "Yes, I like you." For some reason, it was like she couldn't lie to him. There was something in Darrien's eyes that made her trust him.

Darrien was relieved. He knew she liked him but hearing her say it was all the validation he needed. A part of him was afraid to pursue Bishop Lawson's daughter. They had so many family ties, so much in common. If things didn't work out, it wasn't like they would never see each other again. Her dad was his father's mentor. But hearing her say she liked him was all he needed to hear. Although logic was telling him to proceed with caution, his heart was telling him to conquer all.

He leaned in and gave her a gentle, loving kiss on the forehead in efforts to calm her fears. "I like you, too," Darrien confessed, "You're safe with me."

Darrien and Shyanne sat in the car for hours talking, laughing, and giggling. By the time Rashawn, the driver pulled up to Shyanne's duplex, it was almost three o'clock in the morning.

"I am going to be so mad at myself in the morning," Shyanne said, as she rubbed her eyes. "Dang, I forgot I had on makeup." She said, observing the eyeshadow that had rubbed off on her index finger.

"You don't need it," Darrien said, as he traced the perimeter of her face with his finger.

"Thank you," Shyanne nervously said, as she looked off to the side.

"What's on your mind? And I thought your boutique was closed on Mondays."

"It's closed to the public, but I still have to work. Inventory, packaging, you know, entrepreneur stuff. Speaking of, how's your shop?" She inquired, purposely not answering his first question.

"Man, the barbershop is going well. I'm rarely there physically, but everything is going well. I was thinking about opening a second one and coming up to Chicago."

Hmm... Shyanne thought to herself. *Is he thinking about moving up here? This could be good.*

"Well, I better go," Shyanne said, as she placed her hand on the car door's handle.

"Wait, let me get that door for you."

Darrien got out of the car, walked over to her door and opened it.

Man, this girl is beautiful, he thought to himself. He extended his hand and lifted her out of the car. They walked hand in hand as he walked her to the door.

"This is you?" He asked, wondering if she owned the beautiful duplex.

"Yep, it's all me," she beamed with pride.

"This is dope. Nice neighborhood, too."

"Thank you," she said as she rang her doorbell.

"You got a man over here? Why are you ringing your own bell?" He asked through furrowed brows.

His jealousy amused Shyanne.

"What kind of woman do you think I am? Lisa brought my car back here after church, and I told Selena to just spend the night."

As if on cue, Selena opened the door wearing pajamas, looking as if she had just woken up.

"Heeeey, Pastor Roberts." She greeted him with a smile.

"You can call me Darrien. Hey, Sister," he smiled and rubbed the back of Shyanne's hand.

"Ok, that's enough, guys," Shyanne ended their small talk. "Darrien, thank you for a great night. I had fun," she turned her full attention to him.

"Thank you for being you, my Shy," he said, as he brought her in for a full-on embrace.

The hug was so tight, Selena had to clutch her invisible pearls. Darrien gave her a kiss on her right cheek before releasing her.

"Goodnight."

"Goodnight."

Shyanne walked in her door after Selena and immediately, the two of them started screaming with excitement.

"Giiiiiirl, what happened? Clearly, y'all had a good time because that hug was sinful. Were his lips soft? Girl, what happened?" Selena asked all in one breath.

"Calm down, sus," Shyanne said while yawning. "I'm going to make it quick because we have to go to the boutique tomorrow morning."

"Girl, it's your boutique. We can take the day off." Selena retorted.

"Um, no, ma'am. Bosses don't take breaks. Anyway, he rented out Priscilla's and we had a romantic, candlelit dinner with just us and some good ole soul food."

"Yes, brother, for the private restaurant."

"Yeah, at first, I was scared; but as the date went on, I let my guard down a little. He did tell me he likes me," Shyanne smiled.

"Aww! Be still my heart."

"And I admitted that I liked him. And yes, his lips are soft, girl. His forehead kiss was the sweetest. Anyway, we talked forever. We have so much in common. Then, his driver brought us back here. That's pretty much it." Shyanne said and smiled.

"Well, do you see this going anywhere after this?" Selena asked.

"Yeah, I do. But right now, I see me going to bed. Goodnight!" Shyanne said, as she walked up the stairs into her bedroom.

"Selena! Come get your stuff out of my room and take your tail into the guest room! I know you ain't think you were sleeping in my bed," Shyanne yelled down the stairs.

Chapter 7

T he next morning, Shyanne was so sleepy at the boutique, her eyes kept crossing and she had a difficult time focusing. She was hungry, but she decided to keep pushing through the day. She ordered new pieces for the boutique, dressed the mannequins and met with the event planners for the Pizazz fashion show. Meanwhile, Selena did the inventory, which was a day-long job.

Selena loved her little sister, Shyanne, and was very pleased to know that she was starting to like someone. Shyanne never had much luck in the dating department. Selena just couldn't understand why. Her sister was smart, sweet, a little naïve, but she loved God and was a genuine person.

Selena always thought it was her job to protect her sister. Although Shyanne was the sister with her own business and had a vision, Selena was her biggest cheerleader. They were two different people. Although Selena was the oldest, Shyanne acted older. She was the first to leave their parents' house, and she always wanted to take care of everyone else. Heck, Selena worked for her sister.

Selena was 5'9", just an inch shorter than her sister. She had pecan colored, dewy skin, thick eyebrows, and full lips. Her deep-set, hazel eyes were her best feature. She was a solid size 10. She had some junk in the trunk, but she wasn't slugging like Shyanne; however, she was top-heavier than her sister. Selena wore a D-cup bra and knew she had it going on.

She, unlike Shyanne, loved sports. Selena loved basketball and just knew that she was destined to marry Kevin Durant. Even her boyfriend, Kyle, knew that Kevin was the true love of her life.

Kyle was a musician at their church—a keyboardist. He was two inches shorter than Selena, but she didn't mind. She loved that little man. They'd been together for two years. Selena wondered when she would get a ring. She was twenty-seven years old and wanted to get married before she turned thirty.

Selena, like Shyanne, was still a virgin. Kyle was not. Although he assured her that he would wait for her, Selena often wondered if Kyle was getting it from someone else. She swiftly shook the thoughts out of her mind. He hadn't given her any reasons not to trust him; it was her own insecurities eating away at her.

Selena looked over at her sister. Shyanne was the epitome of a hustler. She did whatever she needed to do to make her dreams manifest in reality. Selena was her runner. She helped make the dreams come true.

"Aye, Shy," Selena called out.

"What's up?" Shyanne answered while she worked.

"Are you hungry like I am? 'Cause my stomach is over here wrapped around my spine."

"Um...well, I have to meet with the party planners. They'll be here in ten minutes. We can head out to eat after that." Shyanne said. She was still working and couldn't break her focus just to eat.

Selena was starving. She didn't know how long this meeting was supposed to last, but she was hungry now. Unfortunately, she had to wait for her sister.

As she counted products in the store, she looked over at her sister, who was now texting and smiling. It was clear she was talking to Darrien, which reminded her that she hadn't heard from Kyle all day. Selena went to the back of the store and texted Kyle.

Selena:
Hey babe!

Maybe he can bring me something to eat, Selena reasoned. She continued with her work and decided to catch up with her sister until the planners got there.

"Shy, have you told the girls about your first official date?" Selena asked, being nosey.

"Nope, not yet. I did want to tell them in person. We should all get some ice cream or something, so I can tell them," Shyanne paused, "I really don't want everybody and their grandmother to be in my business. You know I'm private."

"Yep, I feel you."

"But um...Darrien is on his way. I left my purse in the car last night so he's going to bring it by and bring us some food," Shyanne said.

"Yaaaaas, I'm really Team Darrien now!" Selena said, while doing a victory dance.

"He'll be here shortly, fool. He's getting us one of those Chicken BBQ Club salads from Lou Malnati's."

"Ok; great! I had texted Kyle to see if he'd bring me something, but he hasn't answered yet, so this is great. Thanks for looking out, sis," Selena said sincerely.

"You're welcome. He'll be here in like 5 minutes," Shyanne said, getting back to work.

I wonder why Kyle didn't pick up the phone, Selena thought to herself as she checked her phone again.

Five minutes later, Darrien pulled up to the boutique. He rang the doorbell, and Selena buzzed him in. The pair spoke briefly, and Selena went to the back to get Shyanne.

72

"Shy Shy," she called as she knocked on the door.

"What?" Shyanne responded, in a frustrated tone. She was trying to keep it together, but the work just seemed to be too much. She didn't see how she would be able to do her fashion show for her birthday. Things weren't coming together as she thought they would.

"Well, excuse me, Ms. Thing. I just came back here to tell you your man is here," Selena said as she walked off. She understood her sister being stressed, but there was no need for her to get snappy with the person who was trying to help.

Shyanne instantly felt bad for the snappy tone. She was just overwhelmed. She made a mental note to apologize to her sister later. She got up and walked out of her stock room and onto the main floor to meet Darrien.

When she walked onto the floor, she spotted Darrien looking around at her merchandise. *He is so fine. Meanwhile, I'm over here looking a complete mess.* Shyanne did not have on any makeup, and her afro was loose and flying. She had on some gray joggers from Fashion Nova, a white v neck t-shirt, and some silver sequin gym shoes from Shoe Dazzle. This was the one time where her shape was on display. Usually, she had on oversized clothing and kept her body hidden; but today, she was just working. A t-shirt and joggers would do.

"Ahem, ahem," Shyanne cleared her throat, startling Darrien.

He turned around and was taken aback by the presentation before him. He hadn't seen Shyanne without makeup since they were children. And he'd never seen the dips and curves in her body. He knew she was a curvy woman, but Jesus!

Darrien gave her the once over and shook his head.

"Good afternoon. You look beautiful," Darrien said, greeting her with a hug and kiss on the cheek.

"Oh, stop it. I look busted, but you look handsome," Shyanne responded truthfully.

Darrien was rocking some indigo jeans, black and white classic shell-toe Adidas, and a white sweatshirt with the word "KING" printed in black. He also wore a black leather jacket to shield him from the cold weather.

"Thank you," he flashed his megawatt smile, "but you do not look busted. I would rather see you like this than all dolled up," he put up air quotes around the words "dolled up".

Shyanne smiled.

"You don't need makeup at all," he complimented and looked around. "So, this is your boutique?"

"Yep, this is my baby, Pizazz. We keeps the thick girls sharp, honey!"

"I like it. How's your day been going?"

"It's been a mess. I feel like I'm going to break down at any moment. I'm just overwhelmed," Shyanne looked over to the side, so she wouldn't cry.

"Yo, why do you keep doing that?" He turned her face towards him and said, "I'm over here."

When she faced him, he saw tears in her eyes. She was really overwhelmed.

"Sorry," she said, "it's just a lot."

"Well, you're about to take a break to eat then I'm going to help you. I don't leave town until Tuesday night, so I got you."

"Really?" Shyanne perked up.

"Yeah, you're my baby," Darrien said as he wrapped his arms around her.

"Not yet," Shyanne said and playfully hit him in the chest.

They both laughed. Then Shyanne yelled her sister's name.

"Selena!"

"What?" Selena said with plenty of attitude.

"Can you come here, please? We're about to eat." Shyanne said.

"I'm good," Selena declined.

"Excuse me," Shyanne excused herself from Darrien's presence and went to the stock room to speak with her sister.

"Selena, I'm sorry I snapped on you. The food is here. Are you ready to eat?" Shyanne said.

Selena grabbed her purse and her phone. She was ready to leave. She looked up at her sister and said, "Never again say you're sorry. You're not sorry, you apologize." Selena walked to the door then turned around and said, "don't worry about me. I'll get something to eat on my own."

Selena closed the door and left Pizazz. She didn't even speak to Darrien on her way out.

"Everything is not always about Shyanne," she said as she stomped down the street. She pulled out her phone and ordered an Uber to pick her up and take her home, to her parents' house.

Selena was not one to outwardly express her feelings. She held everything in, in efforts to spare other people's feelings; however, Shyanne really had her messed up. Shyanne was not the only one who was stressed. Selena had been there for her day in and day out. She came to Pizazz early and locked up at night. However, Shyanne acted like she was doing everything on her own. Yes, Shyanne was the boss; but Selena was the manager—she didn't do it by herself.

"I wonder what Miriam is doing." She said to herself.

Miriam was 1/5th of their awesome 5-some of best friends. Miriam and Selena were in the same class in 3rd grade and instantly became best friends. They were like twins. Miriam and Selena were the oldest girls in the crew, twenty-seven years old, and their birthdays were exactly 3 months apart. Miriam's was September 14th and Selena's was December 14th.

Miriam was a 5'6" woman who was fair skinned with a buzz cut. She kept her hair short with waves. She was thicker than a snicker. She had a big butt and a smile.

Selena called Miriam to see how she was doing.

"Hello?" Miriam answered with a groggy voice.

"Hey, girl! Why does it sound like you were asleep? Girl, it's the afternoon. Wake up!" Selena exclaimed.

"Yeah, well, I went out for drinks with a friend of mine last night and I'm a little hung over. So, stop the yelling."

"Oh ok, girl. Well, I was just calling to see how you were doing," Selena said as she located her Uber.

"It's cool. I'm going to give you a call this evening. We all need to talk because I want to know how Shy's date went last night."

"Oh yeah! Well, hit me back later. I'm getting into the Uber now."

"Ok, bye," Miriam said.

"Bye."

Miriam turned over in her bed and looked at her companion. He was asleep, and the cover was draped around his waist. His caramel colored, muscular back looked amazing in the daylight.

"Babe get up," she said, nudging him.

"Yeah?" He said.

"Get up. You've got to get going. Your phone has been blowing up all morning."

"Man, that's crazy. What time is it?" He asked while rubbing his eyes.

"It's 12:10," she answered.

"Last night was fun." He said as he got dressed.

"It was," Miriam said, "will I see you tomorrow before your gig?"

"Yeah," he said. He looked at her one last time and left.

"Lock the door on your way out." She called out.

At Pizazz, things were looking up. Shyanne met with the event planners while Darrien did the inventory. She was so elated to have him help her out. Shyanne didn't understand what was going on with Selena. Yes, she was being rude to her but that didn't warrant her absence. Like, why would she leave like that?

If she didn't have Darrien there, she would have been up a creek. After the planners left and the inventory was complete, Darrien and Shyanne sat in her office eating leftover salad and talking. Shyanne found herself lying on his shoulder. Although she knew he'd have to leave in an hour, she didn't want him to go anywhere. She could get used to spending all her time with him.

For three straight months, they had spoken all day every day, well, with the exception of the day Shyanne decided to play games. But now that they'd expressed how they felt, things were different. Yes, everything was moving fast. But what was understood didn't need to be explained. Something was drawing them closer and closer together.

"Shyanne," Darrien looked down at the beautiful girl on his right shoulder. He was smitten.

"Yes?"

"I want you to be my baby."

Shyanne got up and looked Darrien in his eyes. "Huh?"

"I want us to make it official," he said as he grabbed her hands and held them. "I know it's kind of soon, but I just feel it. I don't even want to give anyone else the opportunity to come in between us. I want to be with you, period. Do you want me?"

Shyanne was speechless. Yes, she wanted Darrien, but she was also scared. Did he want her for real? Or was this just for right now? She didn't feel like he was playing games, but things were too perfect. Way too perfect. She felt like the rug could be pulled from under her at any moment.

"How do you know you want to be with me?" She asked sincerely.

Darrien thought about it for a moment. He didn't want to sound weak, but the truth was the truth.

"Because you look like God to me," Darrien said.

"Wow, King. Yes, I want to be with you," Shyanne said through tearful eyes.

Monday, March 12th, 2018, Darrien and Shyanne were officially a couple. Neither of them could be any happier.

Chapter 8

The next day, Shyanne got in touch with her sister and apologized. Selena seemed to have accepted it, but she hadn't been back to the boutique yet. Selena was in her own world. She could not get her mood together. Something inside of her was telling her Kyle was cheating on her.

She had blown up his phone all day yesterday to no avail. Kyle was the type of man who always had his phone in his hand. Even when they were on dates, he had his phone. She almost thought he was in trouble or in trauma; but according to the Facebook Messenger app, Kyle was logged on to social media 1 hour ago.

I'ma try to call this fool one more time before I track his iPhone! Selena thought to herself.

As if on cue, Kyle answered the phone on the second ring.

"Hello," he answered.

"Really, Kyle?"

"Really, what?" Kyle asked playing mind games with Selena.

"Stop playing with me, Kyle," Selena commanded through clenched teeth.

"I don't know what you're talking about," Kyle laughed and continued his mind games.

"Listen, I don't know why you keep playing or why you refused to answer the phone yesterday because if the shoe was on the other foot, you wouldn't appreciate that," Selena reasoned.

She was right. Kyle would not and could not deal if Selena had treated him the way he did her. The fact is that he couldn't help himself. He was trying his best not to act guilty, but he was guilty. To avoid hurting her feelings, he just ignored her. He was sure ignoring Selena would piss her off, but he wasn't trying to hurt her with his secrets.

"I'm sorry," he said.

"Thank you. I just wanted to hear your voice. When you didn't answer the phone, it really worried me," Selena said solemnly.

"I forgive you. Anyway, don't you have a rehearsal you need to be at?" Selena said while watching her wristwatch.

"Yes, babe. I'm on my way to the church to rehearse with the band." Kyle said to Selena.

Meanwhile, as he was talking to Selena, a perfectly manicured hand rubbed his back and kissed his neck.

"Beautiful, let me call you back after rehearsal," Kyle said.

"Ok; don't forget. Have a great day, baby," Selena said.

"One," Kyle said, hanging up the phone.

"Aye, I'm about to go," Kyle said as he placed a deep, passionate kiss on Miriam's lips. Their tongues danced around, exploring each other's mouths.

"Can't we get just five more minutes?" Miriam begged. She was trying to pull him back into their bed. They'd been messing around for two months behind Selena's back. Although Miriam never meant for it to happen this way, she was in love with Kyle. On the contrary, for Kyle, Miriam was just an itch that needed to be scratched.

"Naw, I got to be at Freedom for rehearsal. I'll catch you Sunday night after broadcast though," he said as he got up to leave.

"Today is Tuesday. I can't see you until Sunday?" Miriam asked. Her heart was feeling like it was about to break.

"What?" He quizzed, looking at Miriam as if she'd lost her mind.

"I'm just saying that I would miss you by Sunday and that's a long time to not see or speak to Daddy." Miriam got out of the bed as naked as the day she was born, and walked over to Kyle. She placed his hands on her buttocks and said, "I'm just going to miss you, that's all."

That confirmed it. Kyle felt like she was falling for him, but this was too much. Had Miriam lost her mind? They were not a couple. She did not have his heart. Selena did. Miriam could never be his girl. She was just willing to give him what Selena was not—sex. He felt like a jerk for messing around on Selena. He knew she would kill him if she ever found out. This thing between Kyle and Miriam was supposed to be a one-time thing. But she got clingy. Kyle only continued this affair out of fear that Miriam would one day tell Selena. He had to put her in check though. There was no way she should be catching feelings.

"Aye," he said as he removed his hands from her buttocks. "You gotta chill. You're not my girl," he sternly reminded her.

Miriam stepped back, stunned. She knew she wasn't his girlfriend, but she didn't expect him to shoot her down. She knew what they were doing was wrong, but she couldn't help how her heart felt.

Miriam grabbed her pink, silk robe, put it on and sat down on the side of her bed.

"Go. And lock my door on your way out, clown!"

84

Kyle paused and did exactly what he was told.

Across town at Shyanne's Midtown duplex sat Shyanne, Selena, Kyra, and Lisa. Shyanne had cooked and invited all the girls over, so she could tell them her good news.

"Ok, girls. Get comfortable. Where's Miriam?" Shyanne asked.

"I don't know where she is, but I hope she comes soon so we can eat. I'm hungry," Kyra said.

"Kyra, you didn't cook for you and the Good Reverend before you left home?" Selena asked.

"I cooked our dinner this morning when I got Shy's message. All he has to do is heat it up. I got here straight from work, so I knew I wouldn't have time to stop by my house all the way in Naperville," Kyra said.

"See, that's why I'm the satisfied single of the group. I don't have time to be making folks' meals, but I'll let him pay for mine," Lisa giggled and said.

"Girl, bye," Kyra defended, "You don't want a man because you're scared. It has nothing to do with fixing plates. When you find a man who becomes one with you, cherishes you, loves you, will go hard for you, and is your best friend, you'll know that fixing his plate is the least of what you'll do for him."

"That is true," Shyanne said.

"But everybody doesn't want to be Martha Stewart, Kyra, and Shyanne. Don't judge me for wanting to be single," Lisa said.

"Girl don't judge me for being a good wife and I won't," Kyra counted.

"Ok, Mary and Martha. Cut it out." Shyanne had to step in and referee.

"Did Miriam respond to the group text? Cause it's not like her to be this late," Selena said.

"I don't think so. Call her," Shyanne instructed.

"I'm going to dial her right now." Selena picked up her phone and called Miriam.

"Hello?" Miriam answered.

"Hey, Best. Are you coming over Shyanne's house? We're all trying to wait until you get here to eat."

"Um...I completely forgot. I'm about to head that way," Miriam said.

"Are you ok? Why does it sound like you've been crying?" Selena asked, worried.

"I'm a little stressed. I got man problems. You know, with that new guy I told you I was dating?"

"Oh ok. Well, girl, join the club," Selena said referring to her suspicions concerning Kyle. Little did she know Miriam was referring to the same thing. "Anyway, how long will it take you to get here?"

"10 minutes tops. I'm already dressed," Miriam lied. She still needed to shower and get dressed.

"Ok, Best Friend. See you when you get here," Selena said.

"Bye."

"Well, that was Miriam. She said she forgot. She should be here in 10 minutes," Selena informed the girls.

"Ok, well, can we eat? I can't be here all night, I have a husband to go home to." Kyra emphasized the word husband and cut her eyes at Lisa.

"Yes, let's eat. Kyra has drawers to wash at home," Lisa clapped back.

"Go wash your hands and fix your own plates. Y'all know I ain't fixing them. The honey glazed baked chicken is in the oven, corn and mashed potatoes are on the stove, and the salad is on the island," Shyanne said as she sat down in the dining room.

The ladies got their food and joined Shy in the dining room. Shyanne's dining room was fit for a palace. She had a long, rectangular marble and gold table, which sat 8 people. On the table were gold plate settings and flatware. She had white napkins

87

with gold napkin rings. Her eight chairs looked like gold and white thrones, fit for a queen. The focal point of the room was a French Provincial 4-Door/ 5-Drawer China Cabinet. It was vintage and beautiful. A white, faux fur rug graced the hardwood floor underneath the table.

Kyra prayed over the food and all the ladies ate and talked with full faces. They loved when Shyanne cooked. Whenever she did, the food was guaranteed to be good.

Fifteen minutes into their conversation, Shyanne's door begins to ring. It was Miriam.

"What's the password?" Shyanne said.

Miriam began to use her fist and hand to play the "Grinding" by Clipse featuring Pharrell. Shyanne fell out laughing and invited Miriam in.

"Hang your coat up in the closet," Shyanne instructed.

"Miss. Aren't you supposed to hang my coat up for me? I'm a guest."

"Girl, hang your own dang coat up. You ain't nobody's guest."

"Well, I never," Miriam said, pretending to be appalled.

"And you won't. Now, come on and get a plate so I can tell y'all what happened."

Once all the girls were seated at the table, stuffing their faces, Shyanne got all of their attention. She hadn't even told Selena that she and Darrien had made it official yet. She wanted to tell everybody at the same time.

Truth be told, although Shyanne was 25 years old, Darrien was her first official boyfriend. She'd dated guys before, she'd even had friends, but Darrien was the first to make it official. She was no longer a relationship virgin.

"Ok, guys," Shyanne cut through the chatter by tapping her butter knife onto her glass. "Thank you all for coming to my humble abode."

"Girl, with all this gold? This house ain't humble," Miriam said as she took a sip of wine.

"You got that right," Lisa said, high-fiving Miriam.

"Let's give a round of applause to Shawn and Marlon Wayans, everybody," Shyanne shot sarcastically. "Anyway, I brought you all here to tell you that I officially have a man."

"WHAT?!" Selena, Kyra, Miriam, and Lisa shouted in unison.

"Yep," Shyanne replied. "Darrien Roberts, Jr., and I are officially a couple. Now, I don't want this leaving this room. We are both leaders and people don't need to be in our business. People automatically assume that you're having sex because you're dating, but we aren't. We're doing it God's way." Shyanne said with a smile.

"Girl, I am so happy for you. It's like real soon but if you're happy, I'm happy," Selena said, hugging her sister.

"Well, youngin', it's soon. Not too soon though, you guys have been talking for a while now. I just want me and Cole to double date with you two. I need to look him in the eye and say, 'Sir, if you damage her physically or emotionally, we gone get you damaged.' You know, like what Tina Campbell from Mary Mary said to Goo Goo's boyfriend that first season," Kyra said.

"If you're willing to make it official with him, he must be someone special," Lisa concurred.

All the ladies had congratulatory remarks, with the exception of Miriam. She just sat in her chair, looking at her phone, and completely not engaged. In fact, she was texting Kyle, trying to get him to respond.

Miriam:
Hey, just hitting u up to apologize for how I reacted earlier. I didn't mean to kick u out. U know where home is.

"Miriam?" Selena said, startling her friend.

"Oh, I'm sorry. I'm happy for you. I am. I'm just having man problems," Miriam said, as she took a sip of wine.

"Well, what's going on?" Selena asked.

"Yeah, because you're being real quiet over there," Shyanne agreed.

"Nothing. I don't want to bother you guys with this little petty stuff," Miriam said, trying to change the subject.

"Thank you," Kyra whispered under her breath.

"Naw, friend. You can talk to us." Selena encouraged her friend to let it out. Selena suffered from severe stomach pains every time she was stressed. It was due to years of her holding in her feelings. She encouraged everyone else to let their feelings out, so they wouldn't have to go through what she had.

"Ok, well, the guy I'm dealing with is really nice. He is fine. He has locks, he's tall, muscular, a musician; he's just a good-looking man," Miriam said. She'd had a sip too much of the wine and was hoping she wasn't revealing too much.

"Mmm! Sounds like my type of man," Selena said.

You have no idea, Miriam thought to herself.

"Anyway, he just always seems preoccupied."

"Preoccupied?" Shyanne asked.

"Yes, he always has somewhere else to be," Miriam responded.

"Mmm..." Lisa said taking everything in.

"Have you all had sex?" Kyra asked.

"Girl, why would you ask her that? They aren't married," Shyanne rebuked Kyra.

"I'm asking because I want to know. Have you?"

Miriam looked down and said, "Yeah. We have."

"What?" Selena and Shyanne said, taken aback. Miriam had been telling everyone she was waiting until marriage, but here she was admitting to giving the hot sugar away.

"See, I knew it. I could tell by the way you've been walking and your skin that you've been getting it cracking. I'm a married woman—I know these things."

"It sounds like he's done chasing because he scored. Either that or he has a woman. Those are the only two times a man will act preoccupied when you're giving up the box. That's why God wants us to wait until marriage. Sex changes your life, your mind, your skin. That's why God only wants us to do it with one person. Sex makes you clingy, and you're only supposed to cling to someone you're one with," Kyra said giving words of wisdom.

"Girl, I was about to shout up in here," Shyanne said. "Miriam, I thought you were abstaining until marriage, too. When'd you start giving up the vagine?" (Pronounced vauh-jean)

"Well," Miriam paused, "he was my first. We started having sex about one month or so ago. I didn't mean for it to happen. I

92

was intoxicated and saw him out, next thing I know, I was telling that negro to come over to my place, in my bed. And I just can't get him out of my head." Miriam looked at Selena and hung her head low.

Miriam knew that if Selena ever found out about her relationship, if you could call it that, with Kyle, it would take all the king's horses and all the king's men to put her face back together again. She didn't mean to betray her best friend.

About two months ago, it all got started. Miriam had lost her job. She was working as a teacher's assistant on Chicago's west side. Because of budget cuts, she was let go. Miriam didn't have time to share it with anyone else, she just wanted to find a job. She had recently leased her apartment and didn't have any money saved up for the rent.

The same night she got the news about being laid off, she decided to go to a club called Velvet. A soul singer named, Jenipher, was performing. As she sang her heart's sad song, Miriam went further and further in the dumps. She ordered rounds on top of rounds of drinks for herself.

Kyle was on the stage, playing the keyboard as Jenipher sang. Although he was paying attention to the stage, his attention was divided. *What is Selena's homegirl doing here?* Kyle thought to himself. He knew for a fact that neither Selena, Shyanne, nor their friends went to clubs—they were church girls.

When the set was over, he got off the keyboard and headed towards Miriam. When he was on his way, he spotted a man trying to shoot his shot at her. He stood back and waited for them to stop talking but they were taking forever. He looked up at Miriam's face and could tell she was under duress. The fair skin on her face was beat red. She had an angry expression on her face and her posture was weird. She wasn't steady on the bar stool, she was wobbling—she was drunk.

Kyle walked over there to save her. That's it. But he got trapped.

"Hey, lady. You alright over here?" he asked, as he looked between Miriam and the mystery man.

"Kyle. Tell him to leave me alone. He getting on my nerves!" She said, as she struggled to get off the seat.

"I got her, fam," he said to the mystery man.

"Aye, fam, I was just trying to see what was up with shorty. I'm out," he said, as he turned and walked away.

"Kyle, I want to go home. It's hot in here. Please, c-c-come with me?" She said, falling into his arms.

"What have you been drinking, girl?" He asked, as he laughed at her drunkenness.

"Don't worry about it, Ky. Just hold me. I just need to be held."

Kyle was bewildered but he held Miriam close. His 5'7", athletic build held on to her for dear life. The next thing he knew, Miriam was licking his neck. He knew he was supposed to say something, but he was speechless.

"Take me home, Kyle."

He took her home and came in. Miriam lost her virginity that night, and her soul went right out the window with it. She had officially betrayed her best friend. Not only once, but it happened again and again. She found herself craving for Kyle. She dressed based on what she knew Kyle would like. She loved him. Unfortunately, she was in love by herself because his heart belonged to Selena. Miriam thought that because his body belonged to her, she could get him to fall for her—only time would tell. She didn't want to hurt her best friend, but she was following her heart.

"Hello," Lisa snapped her fingers, "Earth to Miriam!" She said in hopes to wake Miriam out of her daze.

"Yes? I'm sorry, I guess I was daydreaming. Anyway, I'll be ok. I just got a little love jones." She giggled.

"Well, I'll be praying for you," Selena said, "Any man who can't see the jewel you are isn't for you. Skip him." She bowed her head.

"Now, what's wrong with you?" Lisa asked.

Selena hesitated then said, "I don't know why, but I have a feeling deep in the pit of my stomach that Kyle is cheating on me. I can't put my finger on it, but I just got a feeling."

"What?" Miriam said; she was stunned. "What makes you think that? Do you have evidence?"

"Um, Inspector Gadget, she said she can't put her finger on it," Shyanne shot jokingly.

"Shut up, Shy. I'm just trying to help."

All the girls laughed.

"I just know something isn't right. I'm going to get to the bottom of it though. Anyway, it's late, let me get up out of here. I'm supposed to meet him at the gym before I go home," said Selena.

For some reason, hearing that caused Miriam's heart to drop. She was honestly jealous.

"You guys are meeting up at the gym? It's like, almost 10 p.m." Miriam said.

"Um. Yes, we're grown," Selena laughed. "He goes to Phil Fit, his friend's gym, weekday nights after gigs and rehearsals; so, I'm going to meet up with him there to talk for a bit."

"Well, I need to get home to my man. I'm happy for you, Shyanne," Kyra said, kissing her bestie on the cheek.

"Me, too," Lisa added.

"Same," Miriam said.

The ladies hugged Shyanne and went their separate ways. While Selena, Lisa, and Kyra were all smiles, Miriam was scheming.

Sheridan S. Davis

Chapter 9

♛

"Hey, love," Selena said as she spotted Kyle at the gym.

"Hey, babe," Kyle greeted Selena. When she walked in, he was on the treadmill and got off to speak to her. As he walked over to Selena, he wanted to kick himself in the rear end. Selena was beautiful, strong, and everything he could ever want in a woman. Everything from her hair down to her French pedicured toes was everything he prayed for in a woman. He hated himself for letting a piece of tail come in between him and everything his heart desired. He vowed to end things with Miriam right away.

"Listen, we need to talk," Selena said as they embraced.

"I know. I know I've been preoccupied lately. I've had a lot on my mind. I'm sorry. You didn't deserve it. It won't happen again." Kyle then went in for a kiss. The kiss was full on passionate.

As Kyle's mouth attacked hers, she wondered what brought on this sudden apology. She'd rehearsed her speech the entire ride over to the gym with Shyanne, who was waiting on her outside.

Selena broke the kiss and stumbled backward a little. "Well, dang," she said.

"I just wanted you to know I'm all in," Kyle said, as he wrapped his arms around Selena.

"Ok. You better act like it. I'm not playing with you, Kyle. I was almost feeling like you were cheating on me. You better not try me again like this or it's over. You hear me?" Selena asked trying to sound strong.

"I got you, babe. Never again."

"Alright, come walk me outside. I have to go, Shyanne is taking me home."

The pair walked out to the car hand in hand.

"What's up, sis," Kyle said referring to Shyanne.

"What up, fam," Shyanne said, trying to sound gangster.

"I'm chillin' like a villain." Kyle played along.

"Anyway, I'm sorry to cut off you all's hood greetings, but we have to go. Goodnight, Kyle," Selena said.

"Goodnight, beautiful," he said and kissed her on the forehead.

"Aye! Y'all see that person in the window?" Shyanne said.

"What are they doing? Trying to rob Phil's gym or trying to stalk somebody? Why do they keep tiptoeing around the window like that?" Selena asked.

"I don't know, but I'm just going to head to my car now. I don't want to witness the drama," Kyle said.

"Amen, brother," Shyanne agreed.

"Call me when you get home," he said and lovingly touched the tip of Selena's nose.

As Shyanne pulled off, she hit Selena with one thousand and one questions.

"What happened? Why were you only in there for five minutes? Did y'all makeup? It looks like you did. Did you tell him you thought he was cheating? What happened, girl?"

"The answers to your questions are a) We talked. b) Because he apologized before I could even let him have it; so, I didn't have anything to say. c) Yes. d) I mentioned it, but we didn't really go into details, which leads me to e) he is guilty." Selena said calmly.

"Oh, God. Well, tomorrow will probably be a short day at Pizazz. We can start putting on our Inspector Gadget hats on then."

"I promise you, Shy, if I find out he's creeping, I'm going to prison. Not just jail – prison. I'm going to beat the brakes off him and her," Selena vowed.

"Selena, you don't know that woman. Fight your man. He's the one who is stepping out. Don't be fighting her. She doesn't owe you not one thing."

"You're right. I'm just upset right now. Girl, but yes, I'm going to start digging tomorrow. He better be acting right so help him, God!"

Shyanne hoped her sister was wrong about this. Selena didn't play. She always fought for Shyanne when they were in school. Shyanne never had to lift a finger. Selena was the eldest of four, so she tried to fight all her siblings' battles. Selena was nice and all but when she had to, it was knuck if you buck.

After Shyanne dropped her sister off at home, she facetimed Darrien with her car's Bluetooth. It was a busy day at Pizazz and she cooked dinner for her friends, so she hadn't had the opportunity to talk to her man.

"Hey, you," Darrien answered the phone on the first ring.

"Hey, love. How are you? You're in the bed?" Shyanne asked, after seeing Darrien lying down on her phone's screen. "If you don't get across the dang street!" Shyanne yelled.

"Um. Are you ok?"

"Yeah, I'm fine. I'm just driving, and this girl is walking out into the streets like there aren't any cars coming. It's dark outside; what if I didn't see her?" Shyanne fumed.

Darrien just laughed. Shyanne was very sweet, but still feisty. He really liked that about her.

"You are a mess," he said.

"Yeah, yeah, yeah," Shyanne joined him in laughter. "I was calling because I just dropped my sister off at home and I have a long ride back to my place. I figured I could use some company."

"I'm going to need you to not be out so late. But yeah, I'm in the bed. We're going to get on the road and head to Carbondale at 10 a.m."

"Oh," Shyanne said with a hint of sadness in her eyes. She hated to see him go but she understood.

"I wish I could hang with you one more time," Darrien said noticing the change in her demeanor. "I'm going to stay the full week when I come up to preach at your church next month though."

"Really? Ok; I'm going to plan some stuff for us to do when you get here. We're going to have a good time," Shyanne beamed.

"That's what's up. So, what's going on with my Sister? The last time I saw her, y'all were into it at your boutique. I take it that you all made up," Darrien inquired.

"Yeah, that was my fault. When I get overwhelmed, I get kind of mean, and I took it out on her. Plus, she and her boyfriend were going through a little something; so, she's just over everything right now."

"Well, why don't we do a double date when I come back?" Darrien asked.

"That might actually be a thing. I'll ask Selena tomorrow."

Although Darrien was tired, he made sure he stayed on the phone with Shyanne until she made it home. Her ride was 54 minutes long.

"Babe, if you're sleepy, you can hang up. I'll be fine," Shyanne said.

"I'm good," Darrien said while yawning. "How much longer do you have?"

"17 minutes. Look, I can call you when I get home."

Darrien looked up into the screen. "I'm in Chicago right now because the last time you told me you would call me when you got home, you sent me on a wild goose chase. I think I'll just stay on the phone," Darrien shot.

"Whatever." Shyanne knew he was right but didn't want to admit it. She figured she'd explain to him why she played the games she had, so he wouldn't bring it up again.

"Darrien, the reason why I ignored you that day is because I was scared," Shyanne sucked her teeth. "Listen, my heart was moving faster than I was comfortable with—heck, it still is—and I wanted to make sure I wasn't in it by myself. I told myself I would back off and if you chased me, I knew I could believe you when you said you liked me," she confessed.

"Wow," Darrien said, astonished by her confession.

"Yes. I've been in like too many times. I didn't want to go through the whole emotional roller coaster anymore. I didn't want to like you by myself. And now, I know better. I know that you got me, and I got you." She looked down into her phone's screen as she turned into her garage.

"Shyanne, I told you I was feeling you. What did you think I meant?" Darrien quizzed.

"Darrien, I thought you were running game," she sighed. "To be honest, I've had other male friends, and it's been close, but you're my first real-life, official boyfriend."

"I didn't know that. But listen, you mean a lot to me. I'm not trying to play you. I'm glad you got that out of your head because I'm just trying to wife you and get you barefoot and pregnant," Darrien giggled and joked.

"Yeah, alright. No babies for me, Mr. Assistant Pastor," Shyanne played along. "Anyway, I'm home. Thank you for talking to me until I arrived. You can go to sleep now," Shyanne said as she turned the knob opening her front door.

"You got me up and intrigued now," Darrien stated.

"Intrigued by what?" Shyanne mused.

"So, you really don't want to have kids? You don't want to see any little Shy's running around, terrorizing the streets like their mama?" Darrien joked.

We'd make some cute babies, Shyanne thought to herself.

"I don't know. I sometimes think two children would be fine, but I don't know. We'll see what the Lord says."

Darrien and Shyanne laughed and joked until Darrien fell asleep on Facetime. For some reason, Shyanne was still wide awake. It was 3 o'clock in the morning. She decided to shower and put on her PINK onesie anyway in preparation for that night's rest.

Shyanne sat on the bed, grabbed her phone, and started scrolling down her Instagram timeline. The first thing she saw was a photo of Selena and Kyle that he'd posted like two hours ago. His caption read "my baby". *He's so full of crap,* she thought to herself. She thought Kyle was cool and all, but something was up. If Selena had a feeling he was cheating on her, then nine times out of ten it was true. A woman's intuition rarely steers her wrong.

Speaking of men, Shyanne decided to take a trip to Darrien's page. His profile picture was a black and white photo of him looking down as he wore his civic attire. *He's so fine.* She took the time to stalk his social media profile, noticing something very clear, there were too many women liking and commenting on his Instagram photos. She didn't like it. It was one thing to encourage him, it was another to flirt with him on social media. Well, truth be told, the women weren't flirting with him, more like flirting at him—Darrien wasn't responding to any of these women.

It's amazing how many women will throw themselves at a preacher, let alone a single preacher. Shyanne didn't get it. Yes, Darrien was fine; but she didn't understand how a woman could throw herself at any man, especially a man of God. *Aren't they supposed to find us?* She questioned. It was actually sad to see women of God being so thirsty. It's one thing to express interest, it's another thing to be overly aggressive. Something about that bothered Shyanne to her core.

She looked down his timeline to see if she would discover any remnants of an ex or any questionable behavior. She couldn't. *This negro is too good to be true,* Shyanne thought to herself. For some reason, the two of them together felt too easy for Shyanne. He was smart, he dressed well, he could preach, he was fine, he was an entrepreneur, and he really rocked with her. There'd been no bumps in the road. Shyanne wondered if this was the calm before a colossal storm, or if Darrien was a Godsend. Only time would tell.

Chapter 10

Shyanne woke up the next afternoon rushing. She'd forgotten to put her phone on its charger the night before. *That's what I get for lurking on the Internet all night!* She tried to get herself together to go downtown to her boutique, but she was having the hardest time getting ready. Every time she tried to hurry up, she couldn't move as fast as she wanted. She felt sick to her stomach, light headed, and weak. It wasn't until Shyanne regurgitated after eating her breakfast that she realized what these symptoms were. "That time" of the month was coming. Upon coming to this realization, she called Selena to let her know she was not able to come into Pizazz.

"Good morning, Pizazz," Selena answered the phone in an overly bubbly voice.

"Hello?" Shyanne said groggily.

"Oh. Hey, Shyanne. Where are you? Why do you sound like that?" Selena quizzed.

"Girl, I think I'm coming on," Shyanne acknowledged.

"Probably, because I just ended mine a few days ago," Selena said matter-of-factly.

"Hated it," Shyanne said, imitating the Men on Film from In Living Color. "Can you come and rub my back?"

This girl is so dang spoiled, Selena thought to herself. "Rub your back? Who's going to stay at your store, lil girl?"

"Selena, you are only 11 months older than me. Quit playing. Leave Kirsten on the register and come on. She can handle being there by herself." When Shyanne didn't get a response, she resorted to begging, "Please? I wouldn't just let you be in pain and not help you out. Come on, sis!"

Selena sighed. "Fine, you big baby. I'm on my way." Selena said and hung up.

"Kirsten?" Selena called out.

"Yes?"

"Can you come to the back for a moment?"

Kirsten was an 18-year-old freshman at Columbia College and employee at Pizazz. She was a member of Selena and Shyanne's church, Freedom Temple. Kirsten always looked up to the Lawson family, and they treated her like a member of their extended family.

When Kirsten finished up with her customer, she met Selena in the stock room.

"What's up, Selena?"

110

"Listen, I have to leave and go deal with a family situation," Selena informed Kirsten.

"Oh, is everything ok? How's Bishop and First Lady?" Kirsten was genuinely concerned.

"Oh no, they're ok," Selena said, realizing her choice of words had caused Kirsten to worry.

"Whew!" Kirsten said and whipped her brow, "you know I don't play about Bishop. Ok, well, what do you need me to do?"

"I need you to basically man the register and then lock up at 8 p.m. Now, I'm going to have my phone on, so you can call me at any moment if you have questions." Selena took her key off the key ring, "here's the key. Make sure every single light is off; ok?"

"I got you," Kirsten said like a young soldier.

"We trust you, Kirsten, don't let us down. Now, go back out there and work it, Little Miss Pizazz," Selena said as she patted Kirsten on the back and ushered her onto the main floor.

Once Selena saw that Kirsten was doing fine, she logged onto her Uber app and ordered a ride to Shyanne's house. The app notified her that her ride was four minutes away. Selena sat down in her office and took a breather before it came. She was truly stressed. She knew that once she crossed the threshold to Shyanne's downtown home, she'd be thrust right into big sister mode; but she had her own problems. Problem number one was Kyle.

Kyle's behavior had not slipped Selena's mind in the least bit. He'd been on his best behavior since she'd met up with him at the gym the day before, but that didn't erase his foul behavior from weeks prior. Selena was a woman of her word—she was going to get to the bottom of it today!

The vibrations from Selena's phone interrupted her thoughts. It was her Uber driver informing her that he was outside. She grabbed her tan Coach bag and headed out of the office.

"See you later, Kirsten. Call me if you have questions," she yelled, as she walked out of the front door.

"See you!" Kirsten responded.

Selena grabbed the hood of her coat and held it tight. The heavy Chicago winds had smacked her in the face, pushing her frame towards the street. Selena had a love/hate relationship with winter. She hated the weather, but she loved to dress for the weather. She was rocking some light blue, fitted denim jeans and a mustard color cowl neck sweater. She donned brown leather combat boots and a brown, hooded Steve Madden peacoat. She couldn't afford Gucci nor Prada, but she was always a 10.

"Hello. Selena?" The Uber driver addressed her.

"Yes, I'm Selena. Thank you," she said as she got into the car.

Once she was settled in her seat, Selena pulled out her phone and called Kyle; but swiftly decided against speaking to him. She hung up after the phone rang once. Selena was afraid that speaking to Kyle might cause her to forget all his foolishness. Naw, we can just text.

Selena:
Babe...

Kyle:
Hey U

Selena:
I'm heading to Shy's house. She doesn't feel good; so, I'm probably going to spend the night over there. U wanna meet me there tomorrow? I'm cooking

Kyle:
U cooking? I'm there!

Selena:
Good.

Selena was determined to get answers. By the time she and Kyle ended their conversation, her driver had pulled up to Shyanne's place. Selena thanked and tipped her driver, then headed to Shyanne's front door.

Dang, it! She realized she didn't bring her key. She just knew Shyanne was going to have something to say.

Knock. Knock. Knock.

"Girl, where is your key?" Shyanne said, before opening the door.

"Girl shut up. How about 'thank you for dropping everything you were doing to come take care of me.'" Selena retorted.

"Aww. Thank you," Shyanne said, as she hugged her sister.

"Um...you don't look half dead. I thought you were really going through it. You were sounding pitiful over the phone," Selena observed.

"Hey, sis," Selena heard a voice say. She immediately looked around the room. She knew Darrien was not in Shyanne's house.

"Girl am I hearing stuff?" Selena asked, startled.

"No, fool," Shyanne answered and giggled, "I'm on Facetime with Roberts. My phone is over there on the table."

Selena looked at her sister as if she were crazy. *Roberts?* She thought to herself.

"Since when have you started calling this man by his last name?" She gave her sister the side eye, "Hey, Darrien. How are you?" She asked, picking up Shyanne's phone.

"Hey, sis," he flashed his megawatt smile, "How are you?

"Well, I'm a little on the tired side. See, I was at work. You know I work at Pizazz, right?"

"Right."

"Well, I was working until my little sister called me, acting like she was half dead and needing me to come to take care of her," she shot a look at Shyanne, "but I get here 30 minutes later, after paying for an Uber might I add, and this girl looks fine and is talking to you. That's how I'm doing. I'm doing confused and annoyed."

"Excuse me, Ms. Thing," Shyanne interrupted, "I don't feel well, and I still need you. Darrien just put a smile on my face before you came. Right, babe?"

"Right. Sis make her pay you back for that Uber though." Darrien reared his head back and released a hearty sound of laughter.

"You know I am!" Selena joined in.

"Ok; time for you to go, sir. You're supposed to be on my side," Shyanne said. "Give me my phone," she snatched her phone away from her sister.

"Oh, so you got an attitude?" Selena mocked.

"Bye, Pastor Roberts!" Shyanne looked into her phone and spoke.

"So, now I'm Pastor Roberts?" Darrien laughed the more.

"Yep, buh-bye."

"Bye, Mrs. Roberts," Darrien said and hung up.

"So, how were things going at Pizazz?" Shyanne looked at her sister and asked.

"No, ma'am. Why did you call me over here if you were fine?"

The two ladies went upstairs to Shyanne's bedroom and got into her king size bed.

"Girl, because I wasn't. I had taken meds before I called you and they didn't kick in until a few minutes ago. See, look at that heating pad. It's been working wonders," she pointed, "I still need you to rub my back."

"You are so spoiled."

Shyanne turned over to lie on her right side and got under the covers. Selena then crawled to the top of the bed, reached under the covers and began to massage her sister's lower back. Selena had done this for Shyanne since they were little girls.

"So, what's up?" Shyanne turned her head and asked.

"I have so much on my mind, sis."

"I know, 'cause you're real heavy-handed today. What's good?" Shyanne asked and sat up in the bed.

"Well, I told you. I'm going to do some investigating to see if Kyle has been cheating on me."

"Well, have you checked his social media? I was lurking on there last night and I didn't see anything suspicious." Shyanne admitted.

"Girl, you know I'm not on social media like that," Selena waved her sister off.

"You don't know what you're missing! How are you going to call yourself an investigator if you don't even pay attention to the man's social media? 85% of women find their men cheating on them on Facebook," Shyanne said matter-of-factly.

"Girl, where did you get that stat from?"

"I made it up."

Selena fell out laughing.

"It doesn't matter though. Get your phone out!"

Selena took her phone out and put in her passcode. She logged into her Instagram, that she hadn't been on since last year.

She headed straight for Kyle's page, with Shyanne looking over her shoulder.

"You said you didn't see anything last night, right?" Selena asked.

"Right."

"Ok."

Selena continued to search for something, anything, on Kyle's page. She selected each photo one-by-one, used her index and thumb fingers to zoom in, and went to the next photo. Most of the pictures were selfies, pictures of keyboards, and his bandmates. She saw photos of him at various gigs, churches, clubs, weddings, you name it. Nothing seemed out of the ordinary.

"Maybe you're right, Shy. I don't see anything here," she paused, "but my gut is telling me to look again."

"Speak, Holy Ghost! I'll look, too." Shyanne pulled her phone out and began to look at Kyle's profile herself. She was determined to help her sister find out what was going on. Usually, she'd give Kyle the benefit of the doubt; but Selena was just too sure.

"Aye, Selena!"

"What's up?" Selena said while still looking.

"Um, in this picture of him and his bandmates taking a picture at the Wire, look at the girl in the back by the door."

Selena looked very closely. She zoomed the photo in as much as possible.

"Is that Miriam?" Selena asked.

"It sure does look like her," Shyanne said, taken aback.

"She didn't tell me she ran into him. Is this a month ago?" Selena said looking at the date the photo was posted. "Hmm...maybe she can tell me if she saw somebody with him. What time is it?"

"It's 4:20 right now."

"Ok; she should be off work by now. Let me call her."

She dialed Miriam's number. What Selena did not know was that Miriam had been off work permanently for over a month now.

"She didn't answer."

Miriam hadn't answered the phone because she was busy taking photos of herself in lingerie in efforts to send them to Kyle. Miriam had decided to set a man trap for him. She had to get him to see that with her is where Kyle needed to be. She'd gotten dressed in a nude colored teddy that barely covered any of her assets. She added the touch of a nude colored satin robe to go over her fair skin.

Miriam placed her cell phone on her tripod, set the timer to 10 seconds, got on her couch and began to pose very suggestively. Once she got a photo she was satisfied with, she sent it to Kyle with the caption, "Don't you miss home?"

She looked at her phone and saw that both Selena and Lisa had called her. She decided to call Lisa back instead, praying she wasn't with Selena.

"What's up girl?" Lisa answered on the first ring.

"Hey, boo. You called?"

"Yeah. I was trying to see what was up with you. You seemed a little aloof at Shy's house yesterday and I wanted to see if you were ok, friend." Lisa was genuinely concerned.

"Yeah, I'm fine," Miriam lied. She was mentally, spiritually, and emotionally on "E". She lost the job that she loved, she was in love with someone else's man, and the other woman was her best friend. Not to mention, she had not gone one day without drinking in the past 42 days. She was a mess.

"Miriam, you're not fine. What's wrong?"

Miriam sighed. "Truthfully, the guy that I was telling you guys about has another woman. And before you judge me, I did not mean to fall in love with this man. It just happened."

Lisa went silent. Kyra was right, he had a woman.

"I'm not judging you. Listen, everybody judges me. I was the first one in the crew to lose her virginity. I don't want to be married and I'm going to give up that monkey whenever I want to. And I still love God. So, yeah, I am judged all the way around—it's life. I'm not judging you, but I will tell you, you better leave him alone, friend. Putting that type of behavior out there will only make you reap a harvest of foolery."

"You're right."

"And why would you want to be with a man who is a cheater? You ain't in love with him. You just think you are because you done let him steal the cookies from the cookie jar. You better calm all that down."

Miriam knew her friend was right for the most part, but she was really in love with Kyle. She felt like he was supposed to be hers. Miriam didn't know how she'd get him and Selena to see it, but Kyle was made for her.

"And you better hope the real girlfriend doesn't find out or she's going to kick your behind."

Miriam laughed nervously. If the ladies found out Kyle had cheated on Selena with Miriam, they would surely take turns stomping her into the ground, then going back to pray for her recovery. Miriam didn't know how she'd gotten into this mess.

Things just kind of happened. Her life wasn't supposed to be like this; she was a church girl.

After Selena left a voicemail on Miriam's phone, she sat back and continued to look at Kyle's Instagram. There was only one photo of her on there. That was odd.

"Do you think Miriam knows anything?" Shyanne asked.

"I don't know, but I have a feeling she does," Selena admitted. "Anyway, I'm going to spend the night, if it's ok with you."

"Yeah, that's fine. As long as you rub my back," Shyanne said.

"Well, I wasn't planning on rubbing your back. I was planning on snooping," Selena said as she rubbed her hands together.

"Look, I'm going to cook and invite Kyle to come over here. I'm going to go through his phone."

"Um, Selena, don't you think you're doing too much? Like, if you feel like he's cheating, why don't you just leave him alone. Why are you snooping?" Shyanne reasoned.

"Shyanne, I am going to break up with him; but all I have right now is a feeling. I need concrete evidence. I just want to ease my mind and know exactly what happened," she admitted.

"It's ok, Selena. I wouldn't do it, but I understand you need that peace of mind. I got you."

Chapter 11

It was Wednesday night. Shyanne, Lisa, and Selena were at Freedom Temple's Bible Study. As Bishop Lawson taught, he had no idea what storms were brewing in the pews—and in his daughter's heads no less. Selena heard not one word that was being taught. She was only thinking about the setup she had planned for Kyle. Once Bible Study was over, Kyle came over to the sisters, ready to head over to Shyanne's house for some good eating.

Once they got to the house, Kyle was in shock. In the dining room was a romantic dinner for two. Shyanne and Lisa went upstairs to Shyanne's room and listened by the vent.

"Well, baby, this is for you," Selena said with a smile.

"Wow. To what do I owe this pleasure?" He asked.

"I just want to celebrate. We hit a very bumpy road, but you've sworn that you would do better. So, this is a celebratory dinner for us. We're going to be better from here on out.

"I've made a Greek salad, baked chicken with brown sugar, mashed potatoes with gravy, corn, and some wine. All your favorites."

Kyle looked at the spread and got excited.

"Ok, don't just stand there. Wash your hands so we can eat."

The pair washed their hands and prepared for a feast. As they ate, they began to converse and make small talk. Then, Selena began to open up to her beau.

"Look, Kyle, I have to be honest with you; I have this thing in the pit of my gut telling me you're cheating on me. I don't really know what to do with that feeling because I do love you," Selena confessed.

"Baby, I love you."

"I know you love me, but I want you to also respect me."

"Selena, I respect you. You're my queen. There is no one else for me but you. I apologize for being aloof. I was just being a dummy. I thought I was missing something, but all I needed was you."

"Girl, did you hear him?" Lisa asked Shyanne upstairs.

"What did he say?"

"He's going on and on about how much he loves and needs Selena, but not one time did that fool say he didn't cheat on her!" Lisa whispered by the vent.

That notion had not escaped Selena either.

"I hear you. I just felt like you were out there getting some from someone else because you weren't getting it from me. I know you said you would abstain with me, but I'm sure it's not easy because you were used to getting it," Selena said truthfully.

"Well, I'm not gon' lie. It was hard, it is hard, but I love you and I'm willing to wait with you," he said.

Kyle leaned in for a kiss. He kissed Selena so passionately, she was out of breath. She took a good look at him as her chest heaved up and down. A part of her wanted to believe him, but the other part of her wanted to listen to the words he wasn't saying. It was hard. Kyle loved her, but he wanted sex, understandably so; but Kyle knew who she was and what she stood for before they got together and still pursued her. He should've just left her alone.

"Will you excuse me for one moment?" Selena asked.

"Sure," Kyle permitted.

When Selena left the room, Kyle took out his phone and checked his messages. He had several text messages from Miriam. He decided to ignore her. She was begging at this point and it wasn't attractive. As he'd previously told her, Miriam wasn't his girl. He'd made a terrible mistake by dealing with her in the first place. But he'd since repented to God and to himself. He was supposed to be with Selena, and he wasn't going to allow a big butt and a smile to get in his way of being with the love of his life. Kyle placed his phone down on the table.

"Ahem. Ahem." The sound of Selena clearing her throat took him out of his trance.

When Kyle turned around to look over his left shoulder, his mouth flew wide open. He turned his entire body and chair around in one swift motion to look at Selena.

"S-s-Selena, what are you doing?"

"Well, I feel like you love me, but your attention is not on me. It's on those girls who will give you what you want. So, now, I figured I would give you what you want so it wouldn't be as hard," Selena said as she eased down on his lap.

Kyle could not believe his eyes. Selena was sitting on his lap in nothing but a black pair of lace panties, a lace brazier, and a black, sheer robe that didn't cover anything. Her full breasts and toned stomach were on full display. She began to kiss Kyle on the face, neck, and lips. Kyle was in shock.

"Lisa, what's happening now?" Shyanne asked her friend as she paced back and forth on her carpeted bedroom floors.

"Girl, your sister done lost her mind. It sounds like they're kissing."

"Uh uh, scoot over and let me hear," Shyanne said.

Back downstairs, Selena and Kyle were making out in Shyanne's living room. Selena's arms were around his neck while Kyle's hands roamed her body.

"Are you sure you want to do this?" Kyle asked in between kisses.

Selena was not paying attention to what he said, she just leaned in for more kisses. She attacked his lips with a vengeance. Kyle's eyes were closed the entire time—not Selena's.

Although Selena was not paying attention to what Kyle asked her, Kyle took her overly ambitious kissing to mean yes. His masculine hands reached up and found her midback, still kissing her; then, all of a sudden, he unclasped her bra. Selena immediately screamed in shock. She used her arms to cover herself.

"Look, Kyle, I know I said I would do this, but I can't. This is not me. I have to wait until marriage!" Selena said.

"What?" Kyle asked frustrated. "Look, I'm not trying to pressure you. It's what you said you wanted."

"Well, I can't do it. I had temporary insanity. I want to wait. And I also want you to be ok with that. And I want you to wait because you love God, not just because you love me. I just—" Selena paused, "I need a minute Kyle."

Kyle was stunned. Her mood had changed drastically in seconds. He just decided to give her space. Maybe she'd be able to converse tomorrow morning. *This cheating stuff is driving this girl nuts,* Kyle thought to himself; but he'd never tell Selena about his past.

"Ok well, let me just get my coat and go," Kyle said. "I'll call you in the morning," he vowed and walked out.

Selena went to the door and locked it back. She reached around to her back and fastened her bra back together.

"Shy and Lisa come down here!" Selena yelled up the stairs.

Within seconds, Shyanne and Lisa sounded like a heard of cows running and tripping down the stairs.

"Girl, what do you have on?" Lisa asked.

"Please, don't tell me you were down here fornicating on my couch! Ain't nobody got time for that!" Shyanne exclaimed, grossed out.

"No, I didn't, idiot. I just pretended like I was going to give him some, so I could steal the sim card from his phone," Selena laughed.

"YOU WHAT?" Lisa and Shyanne said at the same time.

"I cooked for that fool, complimented him, made him feel nice, made him think I was giving it up and as we started making out, I draped my arms around his shoulders, used a bobby pin from my hair, and opened the little opening in his phone where his sim card is," Selena said proudly.

Shyanne and Lisa were in shock. They really thought the pair were going to make up.

"Shyanne use your phone to Facetime Kyra. Lisa, please see if you can get Miriam on the phone. I want you all to be right here with me as I go through Kyle's phone," Selena said.

Kyra picked up the phone, but Miriam did not.

"What's up with Miriam lately?" Shyanne asked.

"She told me she was having man troubles. Maybe she's out with him now," Lisa reasoned.

"What's going on, ladies," Kyra said through the phone.

"Hey!" They all responded.

"Look, Selena's crazy tail stole the sim card on Kyle's phone and we're about to go through his stuff," Shyanne dished.

"Oh, no! Why would you do that, Selena? If you thought the man was cheating, he was cheating. Why are you going through his stuff?" Kyra asked. She went into the spare bedroom in her house to have this conversation with the girls. Her husband Cole hated to hear all of that gossiping.

"I did it for my peace of mind. I needed concrete answers. Now, if there be no more questions, here's the moment of truth," Selena said as she put Kyle's sim card in her phone.

"Fix it, Jesus," Lisa whispered.

The ladies were all silent as Selena backed up the data from Kyle's sim card.

"Ok; it's 100% loaded. I'm scared," Selena admitted. "Lisa, can you go through it for me?"

"No, ma'am. You need the answers. Either go ahead or just forget about this whole thing; but I want no parts of it," Lisa said.

"Ok, ok. Let me look at his messages," she paused and looked at all the recent names who had sent him messages, "Daddy, Mommy—"

"Now, that man knows he is too old to be saying, 'Mommy,'" Kyra added.

"I was thinking the same thing," Lisa said.

"Shh!" Shyanne scolded. She just had a feeling that something was about to come up.

"Bae—that's me! 'Ignore.'" Selena read.

"Ignore?" Lisa asked?

"Red flag!" Shyanne said.

"Definitely," Kyra chimed in as she leaned into her phone.

"Open the messages!" Shyanne instructed.

"Y'all, my stomach hurts," Selena informed as she opened the mysterious messages.

"Oh, hell no!" Selena exclaimed.

"WHAT?" The other three ladies asked at once.

"You don't miss home? I love you! Are you getting my messages? You belong to me. Don't you miss me?" Selena read.

"Oh, Lord!" Shyanne said. "I'm sorry, sister."

"Selena, touch the three dots at the top right corner of the screen and see whose number it is or if they've exchanged pictures. I want to know who 'Ignore' is!" Kyra said.

The next thing everyone heard was a gasp. The truth had been revealed. Selena's mouth was wide open, her right hand covering the gaping hole, while her left hand held a phone displaying images of her best friend, Miriam either fully or half naked. She was stunned.

"What?" "What's going on?" "Are you ok?" Selena heard every one of their questions, but she was frozen. She could not believe her life right now. She was in shock. She couldn't move. The only thing that changed about her appearance was the tears that stung her eyelids.

"Let me see, sis!" Shyanne said, taking the phone from her sister's hand. She gasped as well and joined her sister in a state of shock. *This has to be a mistake! How could she?* Shyanne immediately hugged her sister.

"Can somebody please tell me and Kyra what's going on?" Lisa panicked.

Shyanne was so angry she could hardly speak. She just handed Lisa the phone.

"I know this trick did not! Is this Miriam?"

"What?" Kyra questioned, "I know you're lying! Screenshot everything and send it to me!"

All of the ladies were in disbelief.

"I'll be a monkey's whole uncle," Kyra said looking at the screenshots as they came into her phone. "She is really begging Kyle to be with him."

"Selena are you ok?" Shyanne asked her sister. She knew the answer to her own dumb question, but she felt like she should say something.

"I... um... I..."

"Well, I am pissed!" Lisa chimed in. "The whole time this hussy was venting to me she was talking about your man? I'm too done with her! I put that on my Daddy!" Lisa seethed with anger as she emphasized the word "your".

"She vented to ALL of us, and about Kyle? I am stunned." Kyra said through the phone.

"Selena, do you need anything?" Shyanne focused her attention back on her sister.

Selena finally focused her attention on her sister. Shyanne was rubbing Selena's back so hard she felt like the skin was going to burn off.

"Shy, can I borrow your car, please?" Selena said just above a whisper.

"Um... How? Where do you want to go?" Shyanne said in an attempt to change her sister's mind.

"Can I please borrow your car? Please?" Selena asked with more authority in her voice this time.

"Listen, Selena, I know you're upset right now so maybe you should let Shy take you where you want to go. We just don't want you to get into an accident. We've all seen Why Did I Get Married, Too." Lisa said trying to get Selena to come around.

"Shyanne!" Selena yelled out, "Give me the dang keys to your car! Don't nobody else say nothing to me! I just saw my best freaking friend's whole light-skinned behind splattered across my man's screen, not y'all! GIVE ME THE CAR KEYS!"

Sheridan S. Davis

Chapter 12

Miriam sat in her lonely apartment in the dark. As her phone began to vibrate, she looked down with a face full of excitement. She hoped the screen would display Kyle's name; however, the smile on her face quickly turned into a frown when she realized it was Lisa, not Kyle, calling. She ignored the call, placed her phone on her kitchen counter and walked back into her living room to have a seat. *How did I get here?* She thought to herself.

Miriam was devastated. Her lights had been turned off earlier that day, and in her hands, she held a stack of bills that were piling up. Miriam had to choose which bill she'd pay today as her bank account was getting more and more decimated. Miriam couldn't even afford to buy the alcoholic fix her body desperately craved.

"God, please," she cried out.

Miriam didn't know what to do. She was totally alone. She would normally turn to her friends in a moment where she felt like this, but guilt had her quarantined off and cast away. Any time she was around her friends, her stomach was pained.

Although Miriam's mind was telling her to do the right thing and leave Kyle alone, she craved him. Even Kyle's harsh words and rejection weren't strong enough to take her heart away from his.

You're not my girl! Kyle's words rang in Miriam's head repeatedly.

"But I'm supposed to be!" she said aloud, countering the thoughts in her head.

The rejection was painful. Kyle hadn't uttered a word to her in days. She'd sent him several text messages per day, sexy photos. She even had an Edible Arrangement delivered to one of Kyle's gigs, but he refused to acknowledge her. He'd even blocked her on Facebook, Instagram, and Twitter as if she were some stalker. Miriam wasn't trying to run him off; she just needed one conversation.

Miriam just wanted one shot to converse with Kyle. If Kyle couldn't see why they needed to be together after they talked, then she would let it go. But Miriam just needed to have one talk with him.

She continued to cry her eyes out, drying them with the sleeve of her pajamas. She couldn't even recognize her own reflection anymore. Miriam would've never done her friend this way. Furthermore, Miriam would never let life's circumstances get her to the point of uncontrollable tears. Her emotions were ruling her; she was no longer in control.

Miriam decided to get up from the sofa and get her control back. Since Kyle wouldn't respond to her, Miriam decided to go to him. Miriam logged on to Instagram to see if he'd posted his whereabouts. *Maybe he's at a gig tonight*, she thought. However, much to her chagrin, once she searched for Kyle's name, she was reminded that he'd blocked her on social media. Miriam began to pace the floor, using her cellphone as a light source. Bible study was over, so she knew he wasn't at Freedom Temple. She looked at the time and swiftly remembered hearing Selena say Kyle would normally be at the gym around now.

Miriam raced to the bathroom to brush her teeth and lightly beat her face. Seeing as though she had to make it to his gym in Naperville, she didn't have much of a chance to do a full face or put on a bunch of clothing. Instead, she kept on her Teddy and put a coat on top. Miriam was sure that after she and Kyle conversed, and she shared her heart with him, she'd be letting him get into what was under her coat.

As she began putting on her makeup, Miriam felt a flutter in her stomach. Something was telling her not to go to the gym, but she ignored her intuition and continued to get ready to see her wannabe beau.

Once Miriam was finished getting dressed, she headed to the car. She pulled out her phone and decided to play some mood music. Sza's "The Weekend" came on. It put the battery in Miriam's back. She drove and bobbed her head, preparing to win her man.

Chapter 13

Selena sped off into the night air. She didn't know where she was going, all she knew was that she was angry. Selena needed to let off some steam. She had all the windows down in Shyanne's car as if it were summertime. Selena's foot was heavily planted on the gas button.

Be angry but sin not.

The scripture rang in Selena's spirit. She hated when that happened. You were responsible for what you knew, and Selena knew the Word of God. All those years of Sunday School, Sunday morning worship, and midweek services were not lost upon her. She knew she should go home. She knew she should cool down before speaking to either Kyle or Miriam; but the more she thought about the situation, the more she saw red—and it did not stand for the blood of Jesus.

"That negro looked me in my face and told me he loved and respected me," Selena said aloud in the car. "Wait, she said she had sex with this dude and he was her first. KYLE WAS HER FIRST?"

The more she thought and spoke, the more upset Selena became. She didn't know how, but she found herself sitting in front of the gym where Kyle works out.

"Father," Selena prayed, "I love you. I don't know what I did to deserve this, but I am stunned right now. I am praying for supernatural strength and forgiveness. Please, forgive me for what I'm about to do. I don't know what I'm going to do but I have to deal with this. And I know revenge is supposed to be yours, but you're not going to slap Kyle, so I gotta step in. I'm asking for protection, so I won't go to prison and don't let my actions tonight have any ramifications on my daddy's ministry. In Jesus' name, amen."

After the prayer, Selena looked in Shyanne's glove compartment and pulled out her small container of Vaseline. Selena smeared a small amount of the petroleum jelly substance across her face. She didn't know what would happen when she walked into those glass doors, but Selena was prepared for whatever.

She turned the car's engine off and opened the door. Upon stepping her foot outside of the door, Selena spotted Lisa's car parked down the street. *These heifers had to follow me!* Selena thought to herself. She decided to ignore them and head into the gym. If Selena acknowledged them, she would have to acknowledge the conscious she was trying desperately to ignore.

If Kyle was there, he'd be over by the treadmills. She walked through the gym. With each step she took, more and more venom pumped through her veins. There his dumb self is.

"Kyle!" Selena yelled out, startling everyone in the building.

Kyle looked in her direction, wondering why her face looked shiny and her voice sounded so aggressive. Something was wrong, but he couldn't quite put his finger on it.

"H-h-hey, baby," Kyle said as he approached Selena.

"When did you start stuttering?" Selena shot.

"Ok, you're upset. What's going on, Selena?" He questioned.

It was taking all the restraint in the world for Selena not to haul off and slap fire from Kyle, but she was there to get answers.

Selena turned her head towards the door and saw Lisa and Shyanne standing there witnessing the entire encounter. She instantly rolled her eyes and focused her attention back on Kyle.

"I have one question and one question only. It would behoove you to be honest."

"Ok," Kyle said nervously.

"Exactly how long have you been screwing my whore of a best friend?"

You could hear a rat pee on cotton—it was that quiet.

"What are you talking about?" Kyle asked, while sweating bullets.

"Do not insult my intelligence by answering my question with a question! HOW LONG?"

"Man go 'head with all that foolishness you're talking. I'm trying to work out. I don't know what you're talking about Lena," he said and tried to walk away.

"How do you get to walk away when you're in the wrong. Like, you're really going to act like this right now? How long have you been messing with her, Kyle? I'm serious! I know the truth! How long?"

Kyle got on the treadmill and ignored Selena. He was speechless. Kyle didn't know how she found out, but he wasn't about to incriminate himself. Kyle was sweating bullets. He was silently praying that Selena would just calm down and they could talk later, but her calming down didn't seem to be in the cards for them.

"I thought you told me you love and respect me. Love don't do that! Respect don't do that! Can you hear me?"

Kyle continued to ignore her.

"I swear I'm going to slap the dog crap out of you!" Selena said, as she walked up to his treadmill and mushed him on the left side of his head. Selena had mushed Kyle so hard that his head swerved to the right, causing him to fall off the treadmill.

"Aye, don't put your hands on me no more! I'm not playing with you, Selena!" Kyle said while getting up from the floor.

"What you gon' do about it?" Selena walked up on Kyle prepared for a fight.

Meanwhile, Lisa and Shyanne were in shock at the entire display.

"I know you better not put your hands on her! I can't believe you, Kyle," Shyanne said walking towards the pair.

"I got this, Shyanne," Selena retorted, "I just want to know why? Why would you do this to me? Huh?" Selena said as tears welled up in her eyes.

"Girl, I know I'm seeing things, right? What are you doing here?" Lisa yelled from across the room.

Shyanne, Selena, and Kyle's heads slowly turned towards the door at the same time. Shyanne's mouth flew open. She was completely taken aback.

Although Kyle was tired of Miriam and her stalker tendencies, he wished he could've saved her at that moment. *What is she even doing here?* Kyle thought to himself.

"So, this is why you can't talk? Because you were meeting up with this hoe?" Selena asked Kyle.

"Um...hey, y'all. What's going on?" Miriam asked none the wiser.

"What are you doing here?" Lisa asked.

"I—" Miriam tried to think of an excuse for her presence but there was none.

The next thing any of them knew, Selena had taken off running towards Miriam. Miriam didn't know what to do. She ran, too. Selena chased Miriam inside the gym, but Miriam was winded and not a match for Selena.

Miriam felt herself feeling lightheaded and nauseated. However, she had to run for her life. She looked at Kyle's face; his countenance was full of concern and regret. *She knows*, Miriam thought. She kept running until she felt fingers tugging at the back of her coat's collar. Miriam fell backward. She was so lightheaded and dizzy that she could barely fight back.

"I'm sorry!" was all Miriam could mutter.

Her too-little-too-late apology went into Selena's right ear and out of the left as Selena struck blow after blow to Miriam's body and face.

"You gon' talk to me about my man?" Selena questioned in between blows.

Selena reared her right hand back and slapped fire from Miriam's face, instantly leaving a hand print on her fair skin.

Shyanne wanted to let her sister slap Miriam a few times because she deserved it; but when she saw Selena kick Miriam in her stomach, she had to stop the madness. They were in a public place and people were starting to record the fiasco. Although Miriam had it coming, Shyanne didn't want her sister to go to jail over the beat down.

Miriam held her stomach, out of breath and broken down. She took what she had coming to her.

"Lena, I'm sorry. I didn't mean to. It just happened." Miriam reasoned, as she used her arms and legs to shield her face and stomach from Selena's rage, which only increased after she saw that Miriam had on lingerie under her coat. She wanted to beat the lace off her!

"You were coming to sleep with him again?"

Shyanne and Lisa walked over to the girls and tried to break up the fight. Kyle had not moved. He was too stunned by the entire ordeal.

"Selena, let her go now!" Shyanne yelled, but Selena couldn't hear her.

"Lena, let her go!" Lisa joined.

The girls tried to pry Selena's hands from Miriam's body, but they couldn't. Shyanne tried to plead with her sister, but it took one of the gym's muscular patrons to come and pick her up and usher Selena out of the gym.

Shyanne and Lisa looked back at Miriam and Kyle in utter disgust. When Shy looked at Miriam, she knew that it would take all the king's horses and all the king's men to put her back together again. She was on the floor, holding her stomach in tears as she laid in a puddle of blood.

Chapter 14

Kyle walked over to find Miriam sobbing uncontrollably. He searched over her body to find out where the blood was coming from. He couldn't tell. All he knew was that Miriam was rocking and mumbling like a crazy person. He'd witnessed the beat down, but he didn't understand what was going on with this girl. She was lying in so much blood that he decided to call the ambulance.

He didn't want to send Miriam any mixed messages, but this was partially his fault too. Had Miriam not come into the gym when she did, Selena would have probably given Kyle a beat down. Looking down at her, he felt compassion. He sat down next to her and wrapped his strong arms around her in efforts to calm her down.

He'd never been so grateful that he didn't go to one of the bougie gyms. The police would've been there at the first punch, but since he was friends with the owner, Selena escaped a night in jail.

"My baby. I'm sorry. Not my baby. My friend. Oh God. Please, my baby," Miriam mumbled over and over. It was almost as if she were in a trance.

Kyle had no idea what she was talking about, he just thought she was delirious. He held her until the ambulance came then he decided to get in his car and trail them to the hospital.

Kyle waited in the waiting room while Miriam spoke to the nurses, giving them all her information. When they asked what happened to her, she simply said she'd fallen down the stairs and did not know who the culprit was. They knew she was lying. However, Miriam did not desire to file charges against Selena, although she had every right to. Miriam talked to the nurses through tear-filled eyes. The nurses had so much compassion for this young lady. She was clearly experiencing some trauma. Once they were done running blood tests and conversing with Miriam, they sent her to her assigned room where she could wait for the doctor. Once Miriam was settled, she asked the nurses to allow Kyle to come to the back.

As he silently sat in the corner of Miriam's room, Kyle didn't really know what to do. He didn't know who to call to support Miriam. He did not know her family and as of twenty minutes ago, she was fresh out of friends. Heck, he was torn if he wanted to be there or not. He had just lost the love of his life over the fact that he couldn't control himself. He had planned on talking to Selena after she calmed down. He knew that tonight was not the night, but he hoped that one day they could have a conversation about it. He did not really want to go into details about what happened with Miriam—he just wanted to move forward.

The sound of Miriam's sniffing interrupted his thoughts. She had not stopped crying since everything went down at the gym. Kyle knew her head had to hurt because she had been whimpering for quite some time.

The two heard a knock at the door and two men dressed in lab coats entered the room. The first was a Black man.

"Hello," he nodded, "my name is Dr. Reynolds, and this is our resident, Dr. Kasi."

They greeted Kyle and Miriam.

"Let's see here," Dr. Reynolds began to read Miriam's profile. "Miriam we're going to have to admit you. Your blood pressure is extremely high, and we need to monitor you. Ok?"

"Ok," Miriam said just above a whisper.

"Your stress levels are really high as well. So, there looks to have been some trauma going on. Now, my nurse tells me you said you'd fallen. Are you sure that's all that happened?" Dr. Reynold's said and glanced over at Kyle.

"Yes," Miriam sniffled and said.

151

"Ok; well, we're going to give you some pain meds. Also, we're sorry again for your loss."

"What loss?" Kyle asked.

"Um...we'll let you two talk about that. You'll be fine Miriam. Buzz the nurses if you need anything," Dr. Reynolds said with a warm, compassionate smile.

"What's going on Miriam?" Kyle asked.

Miriam cried a bit more. He life completely sucked right now. She felt like the ultimate loser.

"Um..." her voice began to shake.

Kyle grabbed her hand. She was clearly having a difficult time getting her words together.

"Our baby was in that blood," she whispered and sobbed.

Kyle was in shock. In just one blink of an eye, his life had changed. He was going to be a father, but he's not. In one day, he had lost the love of his life and his child. Although he had only known about this child for the past minute, he immediately felt the pain of the loss.

As for Miriam, she was distraught. She had lost a friendship that spanned about twenty years, the man she wanted was not hers, she had lost her friends and her baby, not to mention her financial struggles. She felt like she could not get any lower.

All she had planned to do that night is get in Kyle's face, so he was forced to have the conversation with her. She just wanted to let him know that she was in love with him and carrying his seed. In her mind, they would have ridden off into the sunset after he'd heard her news. But Selena and her jealousy had changed all of that.

Miriam didn't mean to cause Selena any harm, but Kyle was hers—they were soul mates. Sure, the way they got together was wrong; but with him is where her heart belonged. The baby is what tied them together and Selena had killed it. Miriam would never forgive Selena for what she had done.

The two of them sat in the silence of their pain, trying to fathom what had just taken place. Although Kyle did not want to press Miriam or upset her, he needed answers. He had only known about this baby for the past two minutes, but he had already felt the solemn of his absence.

"I'm not trying to upset you or anything, but can I ask you some questions?" He asked in a low tone.

She nodded and cried.

"How far along were you?"

"I was eight weeks," Miriam sniffled, "just eight weeks."

"Man," he ran his fingers through his locs, "so, you got pregnant the first time we—."

"Yep, the first time," Miriam continued to cry. "I've been trying to reach out to you because I wanted to tell you. I needed to tell you that I was pregnant. First, I lost my job, then you don't want me, then I lost my friend, then my baby? I just wanted somebody to want me, and I can't even have that."

Kyle was speechless. He knew there was nothing he could say to ease her pain. He just took her hand into his and rubbed it.

"Kyle, I tried to tell you about the baby. I had so much planned out. I wanted to name the baby Khy because it could be a boy or a girl's name. I came to the gym to tell you the other day, but I saw Shyanne's car there, so I snuck out. I didn't even see them tonight until I walked in. I was so excited about telling you about the baby and now..." Miriam's chest heaved up and down as she cried.

"You've got to calm down, Miriam, your blood pressure is already too high," Kyle instructed.

This was the saddest thing he had ever seen.

Chapter 15

"**S**elena, you have clearly lost your mind!" Shyanne yelled at her sister on their way home.

Shyanne confiscated her car keys from her sister and put Selena in the back seat. Meanwhile, Lisa drove her car and trailed behind them. All three ladies were headed back to Shyanne's house.

"I know you're upset; but you straight up took my keys, ain't got a license the first, but drove down here to fight? Girl! I know Miriam had it coming, but Jesus! Did you have to beat her up like that? She was bleeding, Lena," Shyanne vented.

"Shyanne, do you really think I was thinking about a license when I saw Miriam's big behind on Kyle's phone? I know I snapped. I'm sorry. But I would think you could understand why," Miriam challenged, as she looked at her sister through the rear-view mirror.

"I do," Shyanne calmed down, "I just don't want to see anything bad happen to you or see you go to jail over a hoe. A deserving hoe, but hoe nonetheless. God is going to take care of her. Just hold your peace."

"Girl, God wasn't going to get no licks in. I had to handle that part on my own. He can do the rest though."

The two ladies giggled.

Once they all reached Shyanne's house, they recalled the night's events. Rightfully so, the ladies were all still in shock.

"Oh yeah, we need to call Kyra," Lisa suggested.

"No, that girl is probably in the bed with her husband. Leave her alone," Selena said.

"No, Rocky over here," Shyanne said referring to Selena, "just doesn't want to hear Kyra's mouth. Text her, Lisa. If she responds, call her."

"First of all, it's Apollo Creed. Now, go ahead and text her," Selena joined in the joke.

Lisa:
Yo, fam. 911! You up?

Next thing they knew, Kyra was calling Lisa.

"Girl why is there a 911 at midnight?" Kyra whispered, trying not to wake her husband.

"Girl, you missed it!" Lisa said.

"Lord, God. Hold on, I have to go to the bathroom, so I won't wake up Cole," Kyra whispered.

"Girl hurry up because I need to call Darrien. He done called me twice," Shyanne chimed in.

"Anyway, go ahead Lisa," Kyra spoke up.

Lisa was the best storyteller in their friendship group. She was so animated and vivid that you would swear you were there. Lisa stood up to reenact the story.

"Girl, wait, let me put it on Facetime so she can see you," Selena said. "Um, Lisa, you sleep in the bed with your husband with that bonnet on?"

"Shut up, Rock 'Em Sock 'Em. Anyway, Kyra, this is how it went. You know about the pictures on the phone, right?"

"Right," Kyra said sitting on the edge of her toilet seat.

"Girl, so then Lena took Shyanne's keys, got in her car and took off!" Lisa exclaimed.

"No, she didn't, girl! She ain't got no license."

"Exactly," Shyanne said.

"Anyway, so, Shyanne and I grab my car keys, hop in the car, and follow Selena, who is driving Shyanne's car. It was like a high-speed police chase, girl! We ain't know where the heck Lena was going. That was until we pulled up to the gym."

"Don't tell me you ran up on Kyle!" Kyra wondered.

"Oh, not just that. It gets better. So, Lena goes in and starts arguing with Kyle and making a scene. She was so mad she knocked his hat off, mushed him, and made him fall down to the ground, girl!"

"Selena!" Kyra hollered.

"Girl, no, let me finish! That fool never said a mumbling word. He just kept saying he didn't know what Selena was talking about when she asked about Miriam," Lisa said as she rolled her eyes.

"Men," Kyra said disappointedly.

"Right. So, all of a sudden, Miriam appears out of thin air at the door."

Kyra gasped and clutched her invisible set of pearls.

"I don't remember if Selena said anything to her or Miriam said anything to Selena. All I know is that all of a sudden," Lisa paused.

"Selena chased Miriam all up and through that gym," Shyanne chimed in.

"What? I can't take it," Kyra said.

"Girl, Miriam was doing good! She was straight hitting it," Lisa demonstrated what Miriam's running looked like. "Then all of a sudden, she got tired and put her hand on her head, like her head was hurting or something. And out of nowhere..."

"Selena grabbed her by the collar of her coat, dove on her and commenced to beating the brakes off of Miriam!" Shyanne finished.

"What? No, you did not Selena!" Kyra was completely shocked. She knew Selena had a lethal set of hands on her, but chasing her around a public facility and beating Miriam down was a shocker.

"Kyra, I blacked out! I just couldn't believe it. And then, as we were fighting, her coat came up, and I saw what she had on. This girl had on lingerie, coming to the gym to see Kyle. I tried to beat it off her! God forgive me, but I had to get that one off, sis," Selena said as she began to cry.

"No one could have ever told me that I would have ever gone through something like that in this friendship. No one could have told me that. I trust you all with all that I am. How could she do this to me?" Selena continued.

The other ladies were silent. They had the same question. They had never dealt with betrayal from each other. Sure, they have had their share of disagreements, but this was a completely new low for their group. Their friendship was solid for just about twenty years. Now, in the blink of an eye, everything was different. Did they really know each other at all?

Shyanne looked at her sister and friends in disbelief. She certainly thought what they shared was an unbreakable bond; however, tonight, a link in the chain had been broken. As spiritual as Shyanne thought she was, she did not see this one coming. She usually had a strong sense of discernment; but this time, she could not see what was right in front of her own eyes. Or maybe it was the fact that she would not see it. She looked over at Selena, who just looked exhausted. Although Miriam's betrayal hurt Shyanne, too, no one could feel it like Selena did.

Selena sat silently, holding Lisa's phone. She should have been focusing on her Facetime session with Kyra; but if the truth be told, the reality of everything that had happened was weighing heavily on her.

Selena still had not received the answers to her many questions. Why would Miriam betray her over a man—her man? How long had she kept this secret but smiled in Selena's face? How many times did they have sex? Were they in an actual relationship or was this a one-time thing? And as for Kyle – how could he claim to love Selena while he actively betrayed her? Did he ever love her? Was she not good enough? Was she not thick enough? Was she too dark? What was it? Selena came out of her daze and looked into the phone. Kyra's left hand was resting on top of her head. She, too, was exhausted.

Kyra could not believe Kyle, nor could she believe what Miriam had done. The both of them knew better. If she did not know for a fact that Cole would disapprove, she would put on some clothes, find Kyle and beat him up herself. Kyra was usually the friend with the most wisdom (the one with the best advice); but this time, Kyra had nothing. How do you deal with a betrayal of this magnitude? All Kyra could do is sigh and silently pray that God would heal their hearts, especially Selena's. She knew Selena was fragile.

"Hey, Selena," Kyra said breaking the silence, "I have to get off here and get to my bed. Let me speak to Lisa really quickly."

"Ok, sis. Love you," Selena said and passed Lisa her phone.

Lisa, like the other three ladies, was stunned. Lisa was different from her friends. Although she grew up in church, loved the Lord and was a believer, some part of her was detached. Since her father's death, Lisa had been a little lost. She was the most logical friend out of the bunch. She was practical. While the other ladies broke their necks striving to achieve their perception of what holiness was, Lisa was not. She loved God, but Lisa was ok with making mistakes. She did not feel like she had to get married. She just believed in being a good person and prayer. She was not going to abstain until marriage like her friends. Lisa believed in doing her.

Lisa would date whomever she wanted, and she would date however many people she wanted to date at once—she had her own code of ethics. Now, although Lisa was considered more "worldly" than her friends (whatever that means), she would never pull the crap Miriam had.

Lisa replayed every conversation she had with Miriam about her mystery man. According to their conversations, Kyle was the first man she had ever had sex with. That was more grimy than having sex with him in general. *This girl, Miriam, had really given her virginity to her whole best friend's man*, she thought to herself. She wondered how the pair even got together in the first place. Hopefully, in time their questions would be answered.

"Ok, girl, we're tired and I know you are too. We'll chat with you in the morning," Lisa said to Kyra.

"Ok; goodnight, ladies. We're going to be alright. I love you guys in real life," Kyra said.

"We love you, too!"

All the girls had a sense that things were not going to be the same from that day forward.

Part 2

Chapter 16

One month had passed since Shyanne, Selena, Kyra, and Lisa had discovered their former friend, Miriam's, betrayal. None of the girls had spoken to Miriam from that day to this one. A lot had changed in their lives in just thirty days. The season had changed. It was April, and according to the calendar, it was Springtime. The ladies had traded in their Winter coats for brisk Spring jackets.

Chicago in the Springtime was beautiful. When the weather broke, people began to go outside again. Everyone wanted to be in the city's loop, taking in the scenery of tall buildings, opulent shopping stores, and the lakefront. For those who may have been confused, please note that weather breaking is a phrase used by Chicagoans, referring to the ending of one season into the next. More often than not, it is referring to the sun finally providing heat to the city after several months of severe, teeth chattering cold weather.

The breaking of the weather meant more business for Shyanne. Her downtown boutique was filled with people during the Spring and Summer months—there were no breaks, just back to back customers looking to feel beautiful, and Shy gave them just the right touch.

The thirty days leading up to Spring were quite a doozy for the Lawson family. Although Shyanne swore not to tell the girls' parents about Selena's World Wrestling Federation moment when she used Miriam's body as a punching bag, she did not have to, it went viral on the Internet. It was so humiliating.

One day after the beat down commenced, Shyanne and Selena went to choir rehearsal. Upon their arrival, they heard giggling. The ladies were trying to stifle their laughter until Selena asked what they were laughing at. One of the other choir members reluctantly showed Selena the Instagram meme. The caption read, "When you're saved but you still got those hands!" It was a video of Selena punching Miriam and Shyanne trying to pry her off. In the video, you could not see Miriam's face, only her body in the fetal position. Needless to say, Selena was mortified.

"Who sent you this?" Selena asked.

"What happened?" Shyanne inquired.

Selena showed her sister the video and all Shyanne could do was gasp. In 2018, being arrested was a concern but going viral was just as crazy. You can be arrested in the court of public opinion just as you could in the court of law.

Selena and Shyanne had to go home and explain to their parents what happened. They were so embarrassed to talk to Bishop Lawson about what took place.

Bishop Lawson was Shyanne's favorite person in the whole, wide world but she knew her father. Bishop allowed his children to be themselves, but he was also a stickler for holiness. He had lived upright before them and would definitely frown at the thought of Selena fighting because of a man.

After rehearsal, Shyanne and Selena got into Shyanne's car and headed to their parents' house in Naperville. On the way, Shyanne received a Facetime call from Darrien.

"Hello," Shyanne answered.

"Hey, babe," he answered in his low, raspy tone. Darrien's voice came through Shyanne's car's Bluetooth. His voice alone could make any woman forget about anything and everything else going on around her just to listen to him. His voice commanded your attention—it was just plain old sensual—and he wasn't even trying.

"What's up, Love? I have Selena in the car. She can hear you, too."

"Say it ain't so, sis," Darrien said.

"What are you talking about DJ?" Selena asked.

"Lena is that really you on that meme?"

"Yeah, it's me," Selena admitted in a low voice.

"Sis, what happened? That must be why I haven't heard from Shyanne all day. Are you ok? Do you need anything?"

"Man, I'm ok. I need prayer because I'm about to go over my dad's house to talk about it," Selena paused, "do you remember Miriam?"

"Your best friend? Yeah, I remember her," Darrien responded confused.

Selena looked at Shyanne then looked back at Darrien and began to pour out her heart. "Well, apparently, she wasn't my best friend this whole time." Selena looked down as tears began to well up in her eyes. It had been a rough thirty days for her, and she could hardly believe how her life had changed.

"Wow. I did not mean to make you cry. You do not have to talk about it with me. I will be praying for you, Sis; and if you need me, I'm here for you," Darrien replied sincerely.

"Aww! I just love the fact that you're so compassionate and fine all at the same time!" Shyanne gushed as she interrupted Selena and Darrien's conversation.

"Bae, I can't wait to see you in a few weeks," Darrien said. Family and Friend's Day at Freedom Temple's Chicago campus was just 4 weeks away. Darrien and Shyanne had not seen each other since he helped her at her boutique, Pizazz. The pair spoke daily, but it was not the same thing as seeing each other every day. Shyanne and Darrien chatted for the duration of the ride to the Lawson's house. Meanwhile, Selena sat quietly.

Selena was extremely nervous about speaking to her parents, especially her father. Selena never wanted to bring shame or embarrassment to her parent's ministry or reputations. Unfortunately, being a preacher's kid was hard. Everything they did was judged or caused judgment to come upon their parents. If a preacher's kid made a mistake, the parishioners and outsiders would make it seem as if the pastor or preacher was somehow unable to have control over their household. People would openly say, "if your children don't listen to you, why should we?" It's not that the children were not saved, they were merely human. Church kids, specifically preacher's kids, made mistakes like everyone else; you can just see theirs.

"Ok; I'll call you later, babe. Sister, you ready to go in?" Shyanne's chipper voice interrupted Selena's thoughts.

The sisters were in two completely different head spaces. Shyanne's apprehension about this meeting the girls had with their father went completely out of the window when she spoke to Darrien. There was something about Darrien's tone and his calmness that put her at ease. At the sound of his voice, let alone upon hearing the wisdom pouring from his lips, Shyanne knew that everything would somehow be ok. Her sister, on the other hand, was completely frightened.

Selena was the oldest of the Lawson bunch. She did everything she could to please her parents, especially her Dad. Selena did everything she could to get her father to see her. She was very aware of the fact that her father loved her, but she would be lying if she said she had not wished that they were closer. She lived in the man's house, saw him just about every day, but there was some kind of distance between the two. If the truth was to be told, Bishop Lawson was so busy trying to overcompensate for Shyanne's relationship with her mother that he dropped the ball on Selena. Skylar got a lot of Bishop's attention because she was the youngest and raised to be Daddy's princess. Steven, Jr., got his attention because he was the only boy—he was raised to be a prince. Shyanne was the apple of Daddy's eye. She was an entrepreneur and raised to be the female version of Bishop Lawson; they had so much in common. Meanwhile, Selena was raised to be Shyanne's protector—and she had done a great job. Selena was Shyanne's right hand and overseer with literally everything she accomplished. And Selena would not have it any other way. The two had similar personalities, but Selena was more laid back and practical than her sister. You could tell Shyanne was the sheltered sister.

Selena finally collected herself, placed her right hand on the car door's handle, and got out slowly. She had to face the music.

Selena used her key to open the door with Shyanne on her heels. As soon as they walked in, they spotted their parents, Bishop Steven and Lady Eva Lawson. The couple was sitting in their family room, barefoot with coffee mugs filled with hot cocoa in front of the fireplace. They looked adorable in their matching blue, silk pajamas.

Bishop Lawson was sixty-three years old and he looked great. His bald head was shiny and well-groomed at all times. He had a full, salt and pepper beard, and nice full eyebrows. Bishop looked distinguished like he could have been a chocolate GQ model back in the day. He kept himself up and worked out in the gym every weekday morning. He and Lady Eva were the cutest couple.

When Selena and Shyanne saw their parents cuddled in front of the fireplace, they both admired what they saw and desired to have a loving relationship like their parents had one day.

"Hey, Mama. Hey, Daddy," the girls said in unison.

"Hey, babies," Bishop Lawson said as he got up to greet the ladies.

"Hey, Shy and Lena Weena," Lady Lawson said as she got up and hugged her girls.

The four decided to have a seat together on the gray sectional couch.

"Daddy and Mama, Selena has something she wants to talk to you guys about," Shyanne said, which irritated Selena.

"What's going on?" Lady Eva asked.

"Well, I guess, I better spit it out—thanks to Shyanne."

"You're welcome," Shyanne replied with a nod. Shyanne knew her sister and, furthermore, she knew that Selena had the tendency to drag things out to the fullest.

Selena took a deep breath, closed her eyes tightly, and shot out the words, "Mama and Daddy, I got into a fight." Once the words were out there, Selena opened her eye and looked at both her parents and her sister waiting for their reaction.

"WHAT?" both Bishop Steven and Lady Eva exclaimed simultaneously.

"I got into a fight," Selena said as she took out her phone and showed her parents the meme, which had been circulating around Instagram. It had definitely gone viral. Selena was so embarrassed when she saw it on the gospel singer, Lexi's, Instagram page.

"Oh my God!" Lady Eva said.

"Who were you fighting?" Bishop Lawson asked as the meme replayed for the fourth time.

"I... um... I was kind of..." Selena inhaled deeply in efforts to collect her thoughts. "I was fighting Miriam." Saying the words aloud was just too painful. A part of her was still stunned that the entire ordeal had happened.

"Miriam, as in your best friend since childhood?" Lady Eva asked.

Selena could only nod her head and motion "yes".

"What happened?" Bishop Lawson asked slowly as he took deep breaths, trying to calm himself down.

"Well, Daddy and Mama. I had been feeling like Kyle was cheating on me. I talked to all the girls about it, and they pretty much thought I was tripping. That was until I set him up after church on Wednesday night after Bible Class. I looked through his phone," Selena paused as the tears began to sting her lower eyelids.

"It's ok, Lena," Shyanne stepped in to comfort her sister.

"I looked through his phone and found out he had been cheating on me with Miriam and I lost it. Daddy, I lost it," she began to sob. "I never meant to bring shame to our family. I just wanted to hurt her for what she did to me!"

"Oh my God. Come here, baby," Lady Eva said as she extended her arms to hold her eldest daughter as she shook and cried uncontrollably.

Bishop Lawson, on the other hand, was silent. He was completely blindsided.

"I told that boy if he did something to you, he did it to me, and he did not have permission to hurt me. I am pissed off," Bishop Lawson said as he got up from his seat and began to pace the floor.

"And that Miriam! I am appalled. Little whore. I would've beat her down, too," Lady Eva confirmed.

"Mama!" Shyanne exclaimed.

"Girl, you ain't that saved," Lady Eva rolled her eyes.

"I'm firing him. I am not going to keep paying him to stick around and mishandle my child. We can find someone else," Bishop Lawson interjected.

"Daddy, the church's business is the church's business. This is personal," Shyanne spoke up in efforts to be the voice of reason.

"Whose side are you on?" Selena asked through tear stained eyes.

"I'm on yours, of course, but if you don't want your business all out in the pews and in the streets, we cannot be making rash decisions like this," she rationalized.

After a pause, Lady Eva added, "Shyanne is correct. You might be able to demote him, but to fire him would be too obvious and would only cause rumors to spread."

Selena lifted her head from her mother's shoulder. She was tired of her mother and she was tired of Shyanne. *Whose side are they on? How does this man get to rob me of my heart and my closest friend and still get paid by the church that my father built?* The other thought that was going through her mind was how wonderful it felt for her Dad to have been on her side.

"I do not care what people know. Did he care that he was out here living recklessly? He signed a contract and in said contract is a morality clause. He violated it. And the fact that this video of Selena fighting with Kyle exists was all I needed to see. He is done." Bishop Lawson had spoken.

Bishop Lawson fired Kyle. He brought Kyle into his office Sunday after service and terminated him. Kyle was devastated, but he knew he deserved it.

From that day to this one, Selena had not seen or heard from Kyle. She secretly missed their love, but she could not do away with his lies. This entire ordeal was a lot for the Lawson family, but she learned that her father did have her back. She could not have been more grateful for him.

Chapter 17

♔

The date was April 7th, 2018. It was really funny looking outside. The sky was not really blue, but it was also not gray—you know that funky color that makes you not be able to distinguish whether the sun wanted to come out or if it would pour down rain at any moment? Yeah, one of those days. The calendar read Spring, but everyone had on coats. The temperature did not match the season, but that was typical Chicago. Shyanne and Selena were working at Pizazz. Today was a slow day at the boutique, but it did not matter to Shyanne. Today was the day her man was coming into town.

Shyanne and Darrien had not seen each other for what felt like forever. She could not wait to jump into his muscular arms. Their long-distance relationship was tough, but it was honestly what was best for both parties. Although the two lived in the same state, there was about a six-hour drive in between them. Responsibilities like her boutique, his barber shop, and his duties to his church kept them from seeing each other more often. However, today was the day they had both been waiting on. Darrien and his team were coming to Chicago. They should have been arriving at Pizazz in the next hour.

While the whole long-distance thing seemed like a burden to others, Shyanne loved the fact that she was in that kind of relationship. From Carbondale, Darrien was not a distraction. From Carbondale, Darrien did not deter her from her dreams. Yes, they spoke on the phone and they did video chat all day; but having him in Chicago every single day would have been hard. Shyanne knew herself better than anyone. When Shyanne loved, she loved for real. She loved hard and fell quickly. A little space in between the two of them made it easier for her to brace herself in love.

Today, Shyanne decided to be dress-casual in an A. Smith Custom Designs dress. She had her big, long natural hair in a beautiful, curly afro, which she knew Darrien would absolutely love. A cream, turtleneck skater dress adorned her cocoa thick body. Shyanne absolutely loved the dress. It was long-sleeved, fitted at the top and bodice, which showed off her waistline, and from the waist down, it was a skater styled skirt. On her feet, she rocked a yellow, pointy-toe heel.

"Girl, why don't you take those shoes off until the man gets here?" Selena asked her sister.

"Because I want to be cute when he comes, not staggering to put on these shoes. My toes will be ok. I just hope he is not about to take me somewhere that requires a whole lot of walking," Shyanne responded.

The truth was, her feet were already hurting, and it was only 10:30 am. She had no idea what she and Darrien would do. He had a day full of surprises for her, and she was so ready for it. She was even more excited to hear him preach at her church the following day. It would be the day they had been waiting for—the day that brought them together—Family and Friend's Day. Now, she had heard Darrien preach before, but tomorrow would be totally different. This was the first time she was hearing him as her man—she could not have been more excited.

Shyanne looked down at her feet. Her baby toe on her right foot was weeping and wailing but Baby Toe would have to be ok. She wanted to at least give Darrien the presentation. Shyanne's flat shoes were in her purse. They were there for emergencies only.

About thirty minutes later, Shyanne texted Darrien to see where he was. He was at least 30 minutes away, so Shyanne decided to take her shoes off and give her aching feet rest. She did not have any corns, and she wanted to keep it that way. Shyanne, being the statuesque woman she was, wore a size eleven shoe. It was a chore for her to find shoes that fit both her style and her feet.

Shyanne, Selena, and Pizazz employee, Kirsten, were all pretty much finished with the work they had lined up for the morning. Both Selena and Kirsten were so giddy and girlie, squealing with joy for Shyanne's love life.

As the ladies sat at the desk in Shyanne's office, they heard the boutique's front door open.

"It's him!" Kirsten said as she jumped up and down excitedly, looking at the security screen.

"Girl calm down. I'm going out there now to speak. Shyanne put your shoes on and sashay on out to the floor," Selena said as she took charge and masked her inner excitement.

"Ok," Kirsten replied. She followed Selena onto the selling room's floor, excited to meet the man she had only seen from afar.

"Hey, Brother!" Selena said as she greeted Darrien with a friendly hug.

"Hey, Sis!" Darrien exclaimed as he hugged Selena back. He really did look at her like a little sister. When Selena told him about Kyle and Miriam's affair, he wanted to find dude and confront him himself. Selena wouldn't allow it.

"Sis, this is my driver, Rashawn and my armor bearers Marvin and Tim."

"Hey, guys. I'm Shyanne's sister, Selena, and this is Kirsten. She works here at Pizazz," Selena introduced.

"Hey, Pastor Roberts. You're one of my favorite preachers," Kirsten said.

"Aww man. That's crazy. To God be the glory," Darrien said.

Everyone shook hands and got acquainted with one another. They all made small talk and Darrien began to wonder if Shyanne were there. He had been there for about five minutes and she still had not come to see him.

"Is Shy here?" He asked, interrupting everyone's small talk.

"Yeah, she's in her office wrapping up some business. You know your girl," Selena replied.

As if on cue, as she had been waiting for her introduction, Shyanne walked out of her office. Homegirl did not come to play, she came to slay. She had added a gold, Chanel inspired brooch to her dress. She strutted her stuff to the showroom. Her full hips rocked to the beat of the chant "Strangé, Strangé," playing from the Eddie Murphy film "Boomerang," in her head.

You better walk!!! Selena was cheering her sister on in her head.

As Shyanne strutted, Darrien looked on with his eyes filled with a mixture of love and desire. "Man, I'm so blessed," he said aloud.

"Is that right?" Shyanne asked. "How so?"

"Because God took his good time when he made you for me." The two embraced. He began to whisper in her ear, "I've missed you."

"I missed you, too. I can hardly believe you are here," Shyanne said as she inhaled his scent. Darrien always smelled so good.

"Ok; cut all this lovie dovie stuff out. Where are you taking my sister today?" Selena interjected.

The pair broke their embrace and chuckled at Selena's bold nosiness. When Shyanne pulled away from the hug, Darrien grabbed her and linked their fingers. He had not seen her in months. He was not about to let her out of his reach.

"I'm surprising her today; but if you want to join me in the back, I can tell you what the schedule is; you just can't say anything to her," Darrien warned.

"I got you. Let's go to my office. Shyanne, let this man's hand go and stay in here, dang!" Selena joked.

They walked in the back and Darrien said, "I'm taking her to Acanto, that Italian restaurant downtown."

"That's cool."

"Then, we have tickets to the Chicago Bulls basketball game."

"Oh, that's what's up!" Selena got excited.

"Then, I was thinking we could grab some tacos and head over to the hotel to watch movies. That's it. Oh, and I got her a gift for the boutique," Darrien said. He had noticed Selena's face had changed. "What's wrong?"

"Let's rewind. You said get tacos and go to the hotel to watch movies?" Selena asked seeking clarity.

"Yeah," he shrugged.

"No."

"What do you mean?" He asked.

"My sister is not going for that, and you should not stand for that. You all are abstaining. There's no reason for her to be in your room, Pastor. Now, if a group of us are all kicking it to watch movies, fine; but one on one? That's how rumors get started and how tails get hot. No, sir."

"Oh, man. I did not even think about that. Good looking out, sis," he extended his arm to give Selena a pound like it was 2003. "Look, can you order some tacos and stuff? We can come back here after the game and me, you, Shy, Rashawn, Marvin, Tim, Kyra, Cole, and Lisa can all have a good time. I already bought one of her favorite movies, 'Two Can Play That Game!'"

"Oh, yeah. Let's do it."

"Darrien, can we go or nah?" Shyanne hollered out. She had grown tired of waiting and was ready to get on with her day.

"I'm coming, babe," he called out to her. "Let me get out here before the spoiled little lady throws a fit."

"Hey, don't talk about my sister. Only I can do that," Selena said, joking with Darrien. Though her love life had been ripped to shreds a couple of months ago, Selena's heart was filled with hope for Shyanne and Darrien. She had no doubt that he was "the one"; she prayed he would live up to her expectations because if he did not, it would be off with his head.

"Are you ready to go, Love?" Shyanne asked Darrien, upon his return to the sale's floor.

"Yes. And did I tell you, you look beautiful? Cream is a great color on you," Darrien said, as he stared deeply into her eyes.

"You're looking quite spiffy yourself, sir," Shyanne complimented her guy. She was not lying either. Darrien was looking quite casually handsome today. He wore an all denim outfit, which included a denim button up shirt, and jeans. Around his neck was a gold necklace that had a mustard seed in the charm. He also had on a pair of custom, cobalt blue Nike gym shoes. His hair was the same as it always was, crisp and his waves were sharp and pronounced. His beard was lined to perfection, accenting his chocolate skin. The two of them looked great together. More importantly, though, Darrien and Shyanne felt great together.

Chapter 18

Kyra was at home cleaning her house. She cleaned every single Saturday. She loved her life, although the past few months were slightly difficult. The breakup between Kyle and Selena devastated Kyra. The thought of one life-long friend betraying the other was almost too difficult to take in. This kind of deception would make one wonder how long these shenanigans had been going on behind everyone else's back, and furthermore, who else in the group was hiding something. However, Kyra forced herself to table those thoughts and focus on her husband and the friends she had left.

As Kyra began to vacuum her carpeted living room floor, her husband, Cole came in. Cole was a twenty-six-year-old pastor who loved God with his whole heart. He started out preaching at the age of thirteen. All while Cole was growing up, everyone around Cole knew there was something different about him. He did not come from a long line of preachers like Darrien did, but he did grow up in church. Cole went to church with his Grandmother and Great-Grandma every Sunday, every Wednesday night for Bible Class, every Thursday evening for choir rehearsal, every

Saturday afternoon for youth Bible Study, and was right back at it on Sunday morning again.

Cole grew up in a Baptist church on Chicago's west side. He loved everything about his schedule; and while most boys at Cole's age would try to rebel against God and their teachings from the church, Cole lived by them. Well, that is not one-hundred percent true. During his college days, he tried to be "regular".

Cole had gone to Central State University in Wilberforce, Ohio. He had not told a soul on the campus that he was an ordained minister upon arrival. During Homecoming weekend, Cole went to his first college party. He was nervous but excited to attend. Cole had never been to a party before, other than the gatherings that his family would host. This would be a brand-new experience for Cole. He was invited to the party by the captain of the football team. It was an off-campus party at the captain's house. When Cole had received the invitation to attend the party, it read, "Food! Drinks! Music! Strippers! Come celebrate Big J's 21st Birthday!" Cole was excited to have been invited but he was apprehensive about the strippers. Although he was determined to experience new things, he was not going to budge on that one. Cole was an eighteen-year-old virgin, and he wanted to remain a virgin until marriage. He was not the type to go to a strip club or watch inappropriate videos. That's where he drew the line. Once he told Big J he did not want to attend the party while the strippers were there, Big J assured him that the strippers would be finished with their "show" around midnight.

Cole purposely did not show up at Big J's house until one o'clock in the morning. When he pulled up on Big J's block, it was crazy. There were many cars outside, but he could hardly tell which house was his because he could not hear any music being played outside. You see, Big J lived in a suburb where the majority of his neighbors were white.

After an extensive search, Cole finally found a park for his car down the street from Big J's home. Cole pulled into the park, and there was a Caucasian man standing on the sidewalk with a stern look on his face.

"O, Lord," Cole whispered to himself, and to God, after he had gotten out of his vehicle.

"Hey!" The older Caucasian man yelled after Cole in a very aggressive tone.

"Excuse me?" Cole asked. He was both annoyed and fearful. The man's countenance was mean and aggressive. He had on a robe and his arms were folded over his chest.

"If I were you, I would not park there," the man stared blankly.

"What do you mean by 'if you were me?'"

"You heard me, boy. If I were you, I would not park there," the Caucasian man repeated. This time, he emphasized the word, "you".

From that little encounter, Cole could tell it was not going to be a good night. Instead of arguing with the man, Cole decided to just get into his car and park elsewhere. He did not feel like appearing on the seven o'clock news the next day.

Once he finally found another park, Cole entered the party. You want to talk about a culture shock? Cole was completely shocked. He entered the party through the house's side door. He saw some friends of his from the campus and spoke to them. They were all surprised to see him there. They had been in school for three months, and they had never seen Cole at a party before— they just figured he was not the party going type. Cole stood in the kitchen and looked around. There were about fifteen sweaty people in the kitchen getting something to drink from the refrigerator and heading back to the party, which was in the basement.

All the party goers were drinking this drink called "Jungle Juice". When they offered some to Cole, he swiftly declined. No, it was not because he did not drink—Cole was definitely open to drinking wine or a mixed drink here and there—but because of the presentation. The Jungle Juice itself was not in a cooler or in pitchers. The substance was made in a refrigerator drawer where everyone would come in and dip their cups in and drink. There was no ladle. It was nasty. About a hundred college students, including those with bump bumps, were all backwashing into this one container full of this concoction—no thanks!

Finally, a seat in the kitchen became free; so Cole headed over to have a seat. As soon as he sat down, he hears the phrase, "the strippers say they ain't going on unless they get some cigarettes," followed by, "Aye! The strippers need Newports!" Cole was almost ready to leave at that point, but he fought the urge. He had made it all the way there and he was not going home after only four minutes of being in the house.

"Excuse me," Cole said to the young lady sitting on the opposite end of the table.

"Yes?" She responded.

"I just got here. Sorry to bother you but have the strippers really not performed yet?"

"It's no bother; but no, they have not. I told J I did not want to be here to see no harlots popping their butts. He told me that they would be gone by the time I got here, but I guess that was a lie. Why'd you ask? You want to see the strippers?"

"No, I did not want to see them. He told me the same thing," Cole responded, amused.

"Oh. I was going to tell you, you should go downstairs if you want to see those girls," the young lady sniffed.

"Baby, you're looking all tense. You've got to relax," Terrence, who was Big J's older brother, came behind the unnamed woman and began to rub her shoulders.

"Sir, I don't even know you and, please, stop massaging my shoulders. It hurts," she said as she looked up at him disgusted.

"Ok, baby. I'm just trying to make sure you have a good time. I'll be back though," Terrence replied walking away.

"Ugh," she said as she looked at Cole. "So, what's your name? I've seen you around campus and almost asked you if you were a preacher," she giggled.

"Cole. And what would make you ask that?" He eyed her quizzically.

"Because I know ministry when I see it. I'm Kyra, by the way," she extended her hand for a handshake.

The two locked eyes and began talking the night away. Evidently, someone had brought the strippers their smokes because the entire house had the blended scent of sweaty bodies, weed, alcohol, and cigarettes. The way Kyra's sinuses were set up though, she was miserable. Her entire face was aching in pain, but she had come with her friends and had to wait until they were ready before she could leave.

About ten minutes into their conversation, Kyra and Cole heard the creaking sounds of a door being opened. The two followed the noise with their eyes and saw three strippers leaving Big J's room and heading downstairs for their party performance. Both Kyra and Cole's eyes grew wide as saucers when they saw the strippers heading downstairs to the party. Although neither one of them had ever seen strippers in person, they did see some in the movies and on television and these girls had failed in comparison to their expectations. The women did not have on lingerie or costumes, all three of them were dressed in Walmart bikinis that were two sizes too small. Only one of the ladies, the oldest one, had on stripper shoes—you know the kind you would spot in Chicago at Dianna's on Madison? The other two had on flip-flops.

Kyra turned her head and looked at Cole with disgust written all over her face and said, "What exactly are they going to take off if they have nothing on?"

Cole just chuckled in response. He thought Kyra seemed to be a cool chick. The pair sat in the kitchen the entire night, never fully going into the party. Now, even though they did not go into the party, they still were receiving updates from the party. A fellow freshman, some Asian kid named James, was drunk and kept coming upstairs, telling them what a great time they were missing. According to James, the strippers were doing their routine and brought a girl from their school up with them. All three strippers performed sexual acts on their peer in front of all of the party goers. Kyra and Cole were taken aback when they learned this news. But James, being as drunk as he was, could not pick up on their disdain. Instead, James went downstairs to join the party then came back up with more news.

"You people missed it!" James exclaimed.

"James, we are Black. You cannot refer to us as 'you people,'" Kyra informed him.

"Is that racist? I am so sorry, Kyreena. Please, forgive me," James said, as he drunkenly slurped his Jungle Juice and staggered across the floor.

"It's Kyra, James. Why don't you put your drink down? I think you're a little bit inebriated. We don't need you to get belligerent and crazy, right?"

Cole took note of the loving, nurturing approach Kyra was taking with Drunk Asian Kid. She seemed like a solid woman.

"Wait, Kena. Let me tell you. The strippers are out of control. One girl put a candle in her what-cha-call-it, then she lit it, right? Then, she clapped, and sparks flew everywhere. Then, another one put whipped cream in Big J's sweaty bum and ate it. Aww, man," James said as he lost his balance.

"Ok; that's enough partying for me," Cole said. He came, he saw; they could have it. If this is what they called a party, Cole would stick to church.

"I feel the same. James, sit right here," Kyra said as she ushered him into a chair at the kitchen table.

"Listen, Kyra, I know you're supposed to wait on your roommates, but I could take you back to the dorms if you need me to. I know you're over this party, and your face is getting puffy. You might want to take a Benadryl," Cole said, as he cupped her chin with his right hand and examined her face.

Usually, Kyra would slap the dog crap out of anyone who touched her cinnamon colored face; but for some reason, her first instinct was not to slap Cole.

"Um, sure. I'll ride back to the dorms with you; but let me inform my roommates that I'm leaving. I'll be right back."

Ten minutes later, Kyra returned ready to go. "Sorry it took me so long. I had to find them in that sea of sin downstairs," she added with a chuckle.

"Cool. Let's go."

"One second. James, no more Jungle Juice, ok? Your roommate is going to come up here and take you home in about ten minutes," Kyra looked at him concerned.

"Ok. Bye, Kiwi."

Cole and Kyra just laughed.

They walked a block and a half to get to Cole's car. On the way, Cole saw the Caucasian man who had antagonized him earlier. Instead of standing on the sidewalk, the man was now sitting on his porch with his arms still folded. He was still looking as hateful as he looked three hours prior. Cole nodded his head towards the man, who met him with an angry snarl. Cole just laughed and kept it moving.

"What was that about?" Kyra asked.

"He's just a racist, old man. Pray for him," Cole said genuinely.

"Pray for him? You are a preacher, aren't you?" Kyra asked him for the second time that night.

"Yeah, I am. I've been preaching since I was thirteen. Why do you keep asking? Are you a preacher?"

"No, I'm not; but I am a preacher's daughter. My mom is a preacher," Kyra revealed.

"Oh, you know what they say about preacher's daughters, right?" Cole looked down at Kyra.

"Yeah, I know what they say, but everything they say isn't true. And you know your preaching behind should not have been at that party, right?" Kyra looked up and asked.

"But if I had not gone, I would not have met you, right?" Cole said.

"Touché."

Cole took her to her dorm and from that day forward, they were together. They saw each other through trauma, friendship drama, crossing the burning sands and becoming a Delta and an Omega, building trust, abstinence, and mentoring other couples. Four years after their initial meeting, on the day of their graduation, they got married. After the graduation ceremony, Kyra and Cole went to Bishop Lawson's office, along with their immediate family and friends, and they tied the knot. They had been married for four years, and although they had their challenges, married life was good.

When Cole came home, Kyra grinned from ear to ear.

"Hey, baby," she said as she jumped into his awaiting arms.

"Hey," the two kissed passionately. "How has your day been?"

"It's been ok. I'm just getting the house tidy. Do you have anything planned for today? I was thinking about hosting something tonight."

"I don't have anything planned. You know I just left my mom's house, so I'm cool with it. Anything to unwind. Let's see what our friends are doing."

"Well, you know I do not give two apple craps about what your friend Kyle is doing; but I will call to see what Selena 'nem are doing. You know Darrien is in town, so Shyanne is probably busy with him."

"Look, I have not talked to Kyle since that whole thing went down with Miriam. I think that dude is in hiding and I'm cool with that because I'm not trying to be all up in their business. We have enough of our own," Kyle said.

"I agree; but you know I'm going to be there for my girls," Kyra said as she wrapped her arms around her husband.

"Yeah, I'll let you all handle that," he kissed her on the forehead.

"Yeah, yeah, yeah. Go on into the room. I'll be there in a minute. Let me see what the girls have going on."

Before Kyra could get the sentence out fully, she was receiving a call from Selena.

"Hey, Apollo Creed. I got you on speaker. Cole is here."

"Would you stop calling me that?" Selena laughed. "Hey, Coley Cole Cole."

"What's up?"

"Nothing much. Listen, Darrien is in town and we wanted to surprise Shy with a little taco bar/movie tonight at Pizazz. Y'all down?" Selena asked.

"We're in," Cole said.

"Yeah, we were just talking about potentially getting you guys to come over tonight; but Pizazz is cool." Kyra chimed in.

"You know what? Let's move the party to your place so no customers try to come in here buying stuff. Cool?" Selena said.

Kyra looked at Cole for permission. When he nodded, she agreed. Tonight, was the night to party with Cole and Kyra Thomas.

Chapter 19

Although Pizazz was not too far from Acanto, where Darrien and Shyanne dined for lunch, they held hands, lost in each other's presence the entire time. By the time they had gotten to the actual restaurant, they had almost forgotten it was lunchtime. Rashawn opened the car door for Darrien, who walked around the car to open Shyanne's door. Shyanne stepped out of the car instantly feeling like a million bucks. Darrien never let her hand touch a handle—she loved that. Chivalry.

Acanto is a nice Italian restaurant. Shyanne loved Italian food, so it was a big hit with her. For an appetizer, or stuzzichini, they ordered spicy coppa dates, and a mushroom pizza for their entrée. Because Acanto was known for their wine, Shyanne did a little tasting and decided on a sweet red wine to go with their meal. Darrien did not drink, so he opted for a ginger ale instead.

"Bella, what's been going on with you? How have things been since I've last seen you?" Darrien asked Shyanne and complimented her beauty at the same time.

"Well, things have been cool at Pizazz. I'm still working on my fashion show. You know you have to come, right?"

"I would not miss it for the world," Darrien said, as he kissed the back of her hand.

"Other than that, I'm trying to see about my sister. I have had her staying at my house since the whole breakup and beatdown with Kyle and Miriam gate. She just deserves so much better, you know?" She looked directly at Darrien.

"Yeah, homeboy was foul," Darrien admitted.

"Listen, we've never spoken about this, but I have to tell you so that you know upfront. Cheating is now and forever will be a deal-breaker for me. Darrien, if you ever cheat on me, not only am I leaving you, but I'm calling my brother Steve, Cole, my cousin Rico, and Selena; and we'll all molly wop you up and down Chicago and Carbondale. Things will never be the same; so if you want to leave me at any moment, have the conversation with me and we can part ways; but never cheat on me; ok?"

"Ok; lady and gentleman. Here are your dates. I will be back when your pizza is ready. Did you need anything else?" The waitress had no idea she was interrupting a very intense moment. Shyanne had a serious fear of infidelity and she had to let Darrien know he would never get away with cheating on her.

"Yes, everything is fine. Thank you," Darrien said with a nod. He waited until their waitress was out of sight until he addressed Shyanne. "Shyanne Janell Lawson, I am a grown man. Only little boys cheat. I'm not on that. Your sister and Kyle are not us. I want to marry you. I'm not trying to cause you pain; so, please, don't bring Kyle's foolishness into our relationship. Thank you for your threats, but I'm a real man."

"First of all, I'm not bringing their drama to us. I just want to set that boundary, Mr. Real Man. And, please, note that if you want to marry me, not only is cheating with another human unacceptable, but cheating on me with the church is unacceptable as well. Cheating on me with work is unacceptable. Darrien, what I am trying to tell you is, if we are going to take that step, I want to be number two in your life. I am only to be second to God."

"You're right. And I will fight to make sure you're always number two. Can you do the same?" Darrien challenged.

"What do you mean?" Shyanne looked up from her plate. She felt herself getting offended before he even started.

"I want to be number two. I do not want to come after Pizazz, your friends, your dad—" as soon as Darrien said it, he regretted it. Shyanne did not play about her father.

"Oh, so you have an issue with my relationship with my Daddy?" Shyanne sat up and straightened her posture completely.

"No. What I'm saying is—"

"What are you saying, sir?" Shyanne challenged.

"What I'm saying is—"

"It sounds like a bit of nothing to me man of God," Shyanne's head flew back defensively.

"That's because you keep interrupting me. I was just naming things that are close to you as you named some that are close to me. That's all. Don't make a mountain out of a molehill."

"So, now I'm being dramatic? You know what? I need a minute," Shyanne got up from the table, took her heels off, held them in her hand and walked away from the table.

Darrien was stunned. He did not understand how their little conversation turned into an argument. Shyanne was tripping, and he needed to know why. He decided to stay at the table for another minute before he got up to find her. "Lord, these Lawson women are feisty," he said aloud. He took both of his hands and rubbed them down his face. Shyanne and her drama was wearing him out, and it hahd only just began.

Darrien went to the women's restroom. He could not go in, but he knocked on the door and called out her name. "Shyanne. Shyanne, are you in there? Come out of there so I can stop hollering in front of all these people. Shyanne!"

"Sir," a middle-aged white woman snatched the door and looked at him as if he were crazy. "I am the only woman in this restroom. There is no Shyanne here."

Darrien nodded in embarrassment. "I'm sorry for frightening you. I'm trying to find my lady friend. Have a blessed evening," he said and walked away.

Darrien walked back to his table, paid for their meal, and decided to call Shyanne.

"What?" Shyanne answered on the first ring.

"Yo, I don't know what's up with you, but you need to calm all that down. Where are you?"

"I'm in the car. I'm ready to go," Shyanne said matter-of-factly.

"Are you insane? You leave me in a restaurant and then you go play hide and seek in my car?" Darrien was appalled by her childish behavior.

"Darrien, I am ready to go."

Darrien hung up the phone. Firstly, he had to make a mental note that he needed to talk to Rashawn. The second Rashawn saw Shyanne walking to the car without him, he should have dialed Darrien's number—but he did not. Darrien counted to ten and walked out to the car. Darrien's walk was as smooth as if he had music playing in his ears and he was walking to the beat.

When he made it to the car, Rashawn got out of the driver's seat and opened his door.

"Thank you. Please, excuse us. We need to speak in private," Darrien said.

"No problem, Pastor."

Shyanne gazed out of the window. She was ready to go. Darrien had just gotten to Chicago and he had already gotten on her nerves. All she wanted to do was set a boundary and be transparent and honest with him and he had to make it a tit-for-tat situation. He should have just listened. She needed him to calm her fear of being cheated on, but all Darrien did was make that moment about himself.

Neither Darrien nor Shyanne said a word. The only sounds heard was the sound of the SUV's hazard lights.

"Shyanne," Darrien said in a quiet, sympathetic voice, "I cannot read your mind, baby. What happened in there? What's wrong? I apologize for whatever I did. I never meant to offend you. You know I love your father. I was just trying to make sure we are on the same page. Let me know what I said or did so I can fix it." Darrien gently picked up Shyanne's right hand and held it lovingly.

Shyanne continued to stare out of the window. She did not know what he had done, but the entire conversation triggered something in her and she was feeling some kind of way. Him asking her what he did and trying to fix it meant he cared deeply for her and she needed to stop pushing him away.

"I don't know," Shyanne shrugged. She kept staring out the window. She refused to look at Darrien because she knew that if she did, she would break down and start crying.

"Can you look at me?" Darrien asked.

Shyanne shook her head no.

Darrien reached over and gently turned her head to him. Immediately, the tears Shyanne had been holding back began to fall.

"Talk to me, Shy."

"I'm scared," she finally admitted.

"Of me?" Darrien asked taken aback.

"Yeah..."

"Why are you afraid of me? What did I do?"

Shyanne closed her eyes. She did not want to admit it, but she was completely in love with him, and things were moving too fast. One part of her wanted to take a break from him, another part wanted to be with him every single day. She had never felt these feelings before. She felt completely out of control.

"I'm scared because everything is moving so fast and I don't feel like I have control. I'm scared because I've never felt this way about anyone and I don't know what to do. I'm scared that we will end up like Kyle and my sister." Shyanne took a deep breath and opened her eyes. "I'm scared of losing you."

Darrien was stunned. He thought they were in a good place. He did not know she had any fear or reservations about them. When she said she was afraid to lose him, he was stunned.

"Shyanne, I am not Kyle. You cannot let what they went through affect us. We are not going to be like Selena and Kyle. We're going to be like our parents, married thirty plus years, in ministry, and still in love. I am in love with you, Shyanne. You can't get rid of me; God ordained this," Darrien reassured her.

"Wait. You love me, too? Because I was scared because I love you and...never mind. Thank you, Darrien. I love you, too."

It was the first time either of them had openly declared their love for each other. Shyanne felt like a huge weight had been lifted from her shoulders. She promised herself that she would stop living in her head so much and stop holding Darrien responsible for the thoughts in her head.

Darrien leaned in and the two shared their first kiss. It felt like heaven. Shyanne broke the kiss and eyed Darrien's swollen lips.

"Look, um, we're not going to be able to do that too often 'cause um...yeah. If we're going to wait, then you can't have your tongue all in my mouth all the time. That ain't going to work for me."

Darrien cracked up laughing. He agreed. "Do you mind if we continue our date? I wanted to take you to two more places."

Shyanne clapped and shrieked with excitement. "Yes, and thanks for not breaking up with me when I was in my feelings. You're the real MVP."

Darrien signaled for Rashawn to come back to the car. As they pulled off, Shyanne placed her head on Darrien's chest and listened to his heartbeat. As he spoke, his deep raspy voice echoed through his chest and into her ears. Shyanne was content.

Rashawn, Darrien's driver, was bobbing and weaving through the afternoon traffic. There is no traffic like Chicagoland traffic. He was transporting Darrien and Shyanne from Acanto to the famous United Center on Madison Street, which was about twenty minutes away.

"So, where are we going, now?" Shyanne asked excitedly. Darrien loved to surprise her, but she generally hated to be surprised. Shyanne was the type who always wanted to be aware of everything that was around her at every moment of the day— she wanted to be in control.

"Trust me," he said.

Shyanne did not press the issue. She decided to let her wall all the way down. This man clearly loved her, and she had to allow herself the opportunity to be loved.

When they pulled up to the United Center, Shyanne knew exactly what they were in for. Shyanne loved to watch sports, and crazy enough, she had never been to a Chicago Bulls game in person. Shyanne jumped up and down with excitement in her seat.

"Babe, we're going to see the Bulls?" She asked with a huge, Kool-Aid smile on her face.

"Yes, we are. I guess I did well with this surprise?" Darrien asked.

"You did great, my Love," Shyanne said as she leaned over and placed a peck on Darrien's lips. "But let me change my shoes because my feet have been killing me all day."

Shyanne reached into her oversized purse and pulled out some pink fur slides she got from Pizazz. When she pulled her yellow pumps off, she felt such relief as she wiggled her shoes.

"Eww, put them things away!" Darrien jokingly said as he tooted his nose in the air.

"Aww, shut up," Shyanne playfully hit him in the arm, "my feet do not stink."

"Them little piggies smell like they're still at the market!"

"What and ever."

Darrien got out of the car and walked around to open Shyanne's car door. He lifted her out of the car and they began walking into the huge arena. Shyanne had been to the venue before for concerts; she was so excited to get their seats. She wondered where they were seated. Knowing Darrien, they were probably on the first level. But when they headed to the elevator, Shyanne was taken by surprise. Although she was high maintenance, it really did not matter to her where they sat, just as long as they were together.

As they walked, they held hands. Shyanne remained one half of a step behind him as he knew exactly where they were headed. As soon as they stepped off the elevator, Shyanne was stunned. They were walking to the BMO Harris Club Suite. Shyanne had never been inside, and she always wanted to go in.

"So, here are our seats for tonight. Some young pastors in the Chicagoland area reserved the suite to hang out. When I saw they were bringing their wives, I said, 'let me bring mine.' You ready?" Darrien asked. He had outdone himself this time. Those tickets were not cheap. And it really was not about the money. Shyanne had mentioned on the phone that one day she would like to go to a Bulls game. Not only did he bring her to the game, but he brought her into a premium seat.

"I am," Shyanne said with a huge grin plastered on her face.

When the two walked into the BMO Harris Club Suite, Shyanne saw many familiar faces. Being a daughter of one of the most influential Pastors of Chicago's west side afforded her the privilege of getting to know a lot of the ministers in their city. Although they had kept their relationship private, tonight a statement was being made—they were together for the long haul, and it did not matter what anyone thought about it.

Shyanne spotted the Millers, the Johnsons, the Washingtons, the Ledbetters, and many other young couples who worked together in ministry. Shyanne and Darrien walked around the room, greeting everyone until they found a couple of love seats and sat down. Shyanne looked around the room and noticed the fact that she and Darrien were the only two single, as in unwed, people in the room. She hoped she would be able to talk to some of the young first ladies and gain some wisdom about being in love with a preacher.

"Did I tell you, you look beautiful today?" Darrien asked.

"You did. But can I ask you a question?" Shyanne asked.

"Oh, Lord. Is the mood about to change?" Darrien asked prepared for Shyanne's craziness.

"No, silly. It's a real question."

"What's up?"

"You said you love me. I just wanted to ask why or how you know? That's all."

Darrien paused so he could be as honest as possible. "Shyanne, I have been around you my whole life. It was from a distance most of the time, but there was always something about you that made me want to be with you. Whenever I thought about the type of woman I wanted to be with, you were always the woman that popped up in my mind. When you called me a few months ago about Family and Friend's Day, I shot my shot. And I got you. I prayed for God to show me if you were the one, and I got confirmation that you were. Plus, I love your drive, you don't take my mess, you love your family, you love God, and you love yourself. I would not mind having children who are just like you.

And before we connected, I briefly dated a woman in Carbondale, and I could tell all she wanted was to have the title of First Lady. I knew then it would never work. With you, you don't care about being a First Lady—you just want to be you, and you just want me. That tells me you won't abuse the position. And if push came to shove, you would always take care of me. I love you because you're you."

Tears began to fill Shyanne's eyes again. This time, they were happy tears. She blinked the tears back and took a deep breath.

"You want to know why I love you?"

"I already know it's because I'm fine," Darrien offered a grandiose chuckle.

"No, although we are a fine, chocolate couple," Shyanne said as she hi-fived her beau. "But seriously, I love you because you love me past my fears. You have never asked me for a dime. You never let me open a door. You love my family; you're an entrepreneur. To be honest, when I was sixteen, I wrote out a list of what I wanted in a husband, and the only things you fit on that list are tall, dark, and saved."

"Wow."

"What I'm trying to say is, you're nothing like what I thought I wanted, but you're everything I've learned I needed."

They stopped talking and watched the game taking place below them. Darrien loved Shyanne's energy and spirit. She was not afraid to cheer for her team. She did not stifle herself for those who were around her—no matter how loud her screams and handclaps were.

Before the game ended, Shyanne and all the young preacher's wives mingled and took photos. She was excited to be in their presence and to know that they were all genuine; none of them were haters or snobs. They all just had a really good time.

"So, will wedding bells be ringing any time soon?" Lady Miller asked Shyanne.

"Well, I hope so. He really is special. We'll see," Shyanne answered gleefully.

"Just make sure I get an invite, sis," Lady Miller said offering Shyanne a hi-five.

"Excuse me, ladies," Darrien walked over and interrupted their conversation. "I came to get this queen right here." He wrapped his left arm around her waist and stood to her right.

"Yes, she is a queen. You better do right by her, knucklehead," Lady Miller said and playfully mushed Darrien in the head.

"He got it," Shyanne joked back.

Darrien laughed. He was ready to take her on her final surprise of the evening. Selena had already texted him and told him that they were meeting at Kyra's house instead. He welcomed the change because Kyra was the only one who was close to Selena that he had not gotten the opportunity to know well.

"Let's be out. We have one last stop to make for the night."

Sheridan S. Davis

Chapter 20

Kyra loved to host anything at her home. She and Cole owned a three-bedroom home in Chicago's Austin neighborhood. They purchased the home six months after they got married. She loved the house because it was right in between the city of Chicago and the village of Oak Park, right off North Avenue and Ridgeland. They had the best of both worlds. Kyra was not as high maintenance as Shyanne, and perhaps that is why they got along so well. Shyanne needed chandeliers, Kyra needed comfort and stability. However, she could host a great dinner party and make her guests feel as if they had been on a journey.

Kyra had set up her kitchen's island as the taco bar. She called Lisa over to enlist her help for the festivities. Lisa was glad because she just wanted to be nosey. It amused Lisa to see her friend Shyanne gushing over a man, but she was here for it.

"Kyra," Lisa called as they set the dining room table.

"What's up, friend?"

"Listen, I know we're not supposed to say the 'M-word' but am I the only one who is shocked we have not heard from Miriam?

I thought she would at least come back and try to befriend the rest of us or at least apologize. She went straight up ghost, and Kyle, too." Lisa was still shocked even months later.

"I was just talking to Cole about this. I mean I am stunned. It had me questioning all my friendships, wondering if I could trust anyone; but I do pray for Miriam. Prayerfully, one day we can actually speak to her and get closure, especially for Lena," Kyra said. "As bad as it hurts us, imagine Lena. That's a double gut punch."

"Right, that's why I do not even bring it up to Lena. It's sad."

"But how are you doing? How's the single life? I feel like the old married woman of the crew," Kyra giggled.

"It's because you are the old married woman in the crew," Lisa quipped.

"Whatever, trick," Kyra said and stuck her tongue out.

"Dating is cool. I'm out here living my best life. I'm on Tinder, right? I have met a couple of good dates on there but no one I would go on multiple dates with. I'm just out here having fun." Lisa said with a shrug.

"So, keep it real with me, Lisa. You've never thought about settling down? And before you start, I'm not judging you; I just want you to be happy. You see how Shyanne is all giddy and how in love I am with Cole? I just feel like everyone should feel that kind of love and happiness," Kyra said genuinely.

"Listen, what you all have is nice and all, but I like what I have. I do not have to ask for permission to hang out when I want to; I pay my own bills and do not have to share; I love being a teacher and those are all the kids I need; so, to be honest, that whole family thing is not appealing to me. On my Daddy's grave, I'm good," Lisa said and raised her right hand to solidify her swear.

"Ok. I will leave you alone, but I think you just have daddy issues and have done away with wanting a man because you're scared he's going to walk away from you. But ok, sus," Kyra offered an air kiss and walked out of the room, leaving Lisa to ponder over what she had said.

The doorbell rang, and Kyra glided over to the door to find Selena on the other end. Selena was supposed to be at her house an entire hour earlier to help with the food. Instead, Kyra ended up cooking the shrimp, beef, and chicken for the tacos herself. She had not even changed out of her loungewear, and Darrien and Shyanne were due to come over within the next twenty minutes.

"Who is it?" Kyra yelled.

"I know you looked through that peephole and saw me. It's Lena, now open the door."

"No speaka ingles," Kyra countered.

"You already said 'who is it' in English, fool. Hurry up and open the door. I have bags in my hand."

Kyra snatched the door open and peaked her head out. "Maybe if you knew how to tell time, I would know how to let you in," and closed the door back in her face.

"Ugh! Kyra, I'm sorry for being late. Can you let me in?"

"Fine," Kyra opened the door then left to go upstairs to her bedroom.

She turned on the light and found Cole in the middle of the bed knocked out. She slid into the bed next to him and planted multiple kisses on his forehead, eyelids, nose, cheeks, and finally his mouth. His eyes popped open and he was happy to see his beautiful wife lying next to him. Cole loved Kyra with everything he had inside of him. She was his best friend. He palmed her butt with his right hand and kissed her back with passion and aggression.

"You need to get up sleepy head. Our guests will be over in twenty minutes. Put on some clothes," Kyra instructed.

"Twenty minutes, huh?" He asked with his right eyebrow raised.

"Yes, and I have to wash my behind, beat my face and put on some clothes; so that ain't happening right now. Love you anyway," Kyra leaned in and kissed him again, then headed into their bathroom.

Kyra usually took showers for twenty minutes, but she was in a hurry today. She took seven minutes to hit the spots that were most important—you know, the parts with folds and creases, dried off, and was in front of her vanity doing her makeup. Their home had three bedrooms: their master suite, a bedroom that Kyra turned into her Queen Escape, and a bedroom that was Cole's office and Man Cave.

Kyra's Queen Escape looked like a miniature Sephora store. It was decked out in black, white, and splashes of rose gold. She had a black and white striped vanity mirror over her glass desk that she found on Amazon. Over the mirror was a wall sticker that said, "I Am Mrs. Jones". She had a day bed in the corner, decorated with white and rose gold sequin pillows. In the middle of the room was her desk with her laptop, desktop, printer, and her custom black and white chair she got from Kenyetta Brownlee, a dope interior designer and painter on the west side.

Kyra finished her makeup, then crept back into her bedroom to put on some clothes. She looked in her closet to find the outfit that said, "I'm casual, but I'm still the hostess." She found a green, hi-lo tunic and paired it with some distressed jeans. Kyra brushed her long hair to the back of her head and styled it in a messy chignon. She placed gold ear cuffs on her ears and headed downstairs.

Everything looked great. On the island was a fully stocked taco bar. There were soft shells and hard shells, ground beef, ground turkey, shrimp, chicken, sour cream, guacamole, pico de gallo, lettuce, spinach, three types of cheeses, diced tomatoes, diced onions, salsa, and limes available for everyone's consumption. Rice and beans were on the stove. On the counter was 5 flavors of virgin margaritas and daiquiris. Kyra and Cole did not serve alcohol in their home. They also had churros for dessert.

Kyra had outdone herself on the dining room table. She had an array of red, white, and green flowers and décor. Her table was set for nine: Darrien, Shyanne, Kyra, Cole, Selena, Lisa, and Darrien's driver and two armor bearers, whom Kyra had not met. Each person had their own assigned seating with their nameplate labeling each seat. At the head of the table would be Cole, then to his right sat Kyra, then Shyanne, Darrien, and Lisa. Across from Lisa sat Rashawn, Darrien's armor bearers Marvin and Tim, and Selena sat to the left of Cole. Everything would be perfect.

To set the mood of love and light, Kyra went to her television and connected her Apple TV. She looked through her playlist and found the one she created entitled "Love". She clicked shuffle and the first song that came on was "Is Love Enough" by Shakale Davis, who was an artist from Chicago. Kyra began to sway to the beat of the music and had a seat on the couch where Selena, Lisa, and Cole were seated.

"Who is this? I like this little song," Selena said as she began to vibe to the music.

"Well, if you could read, Lena, it says Shakale Davis right there on the screen. Duh!" Lisa answered and rolled her eyes.

All four of them erupted into laughter.

"Shut up," Selena retorted.

"Lisa is a fool. Don't you just love this song though? He's Apostle Davis' son. You know his church is over there on Arthington Street behind Manley High School. I'm proud of him. He's only 19," Kyra replied. She was genuinely impressed by his gift.

"What? The Apostle let his son sing the blues? He is sangin' though," Selena added.

"Yeah, I'm going to add this to my playlist, too. I love it," Cole said.

The sound of the doorbell let them know the party was about to begin. Kyra got up from the couch and headed over to the door.

"Who is it?" Kyra asked.

"Shy."

"Hey, Best," Kyra opened the door and greeted Shyanne with a huge hug. "You look cute, girl! Come on, cream!"

"Thanks, Pud!"

"Hey, Darrien," Kyra said as she extended her right hand for a handshake.

"What's up, Kyra. This is Rashawn, Marvin, and Tim."

"Hey, guys. Everyone, come on in, and please, remove your shoes. There's a basket of socks right behind that door if any of you need some. Once the shoes were removed, Darrien, Shyanne, Rashawn, Marvin, and Tim headed into the living room. After the introductions and greetings had commenced, Kyra invited everyone to move the party into the dining room. Everyone began to find their seating assignment and began to converse with each other.

"Hey, ladies and gents," Kyra said as she stood to get everyone's attention. "I'm going to ask my husband, Cole, to pray over the food, and then we're going to eat. It's buffet style. We have beef, turkey, chicken, and shrimp tacos with all the trimmings, rice and beans on the stove, and virgin margaritas and daiquiris. Eat up and then, we're going to watch a movie. Babe, will you pray?"

"Sure. Father, we thank you for this food and the hands that prepared it. We pray that it will be nourishing to our bodies.

And we thank you for genuine friendship and this time of fellowship. In Jesus' name, amen."

"Amen," everyone said at once.

"Time to eat!" Kyra encouraged.

"King, what do you want on your tacos?" Kyra asked Cole.

"Can I get one shrimp and one chicken taco. You know what I like, Queen. Hook it up for me," Cole replied.

"What do you want to eat?" Shyanne leaned over and whispered to Darrien.

"Oh snap. You're fixing my plate?"

"Yeah, I am. I will fix plates for my man. What do you want?"

"Let me get chicken tacos with pico de gallo, cheese, sour cream, salsa, rice and beans, please."

Shyanne got up and went into the kitchen to fix her man's plate.

The entire crew was killing their tacos. One thing was fact — Kyra could cook her behind off.

"Babe, you threw down with these tacos," Cole said in between chews.

"Thank you," Kyra grinned from ear to ear. She loved the praise she got from everyone at the table. Although she worked in corporate America, it was actually her dream to open her own catering company one day.

"So," Selena interjected, "how was your guys' date earlier?"

Shyanne and Darrien looked at each other for permission to be honest and tell the truth.

"Well, it started off kind of rocky, but we are great now," Shyanne said and flashed her smile at Darrien.

"Well, why was it rocky?" Kyra said.

"Geesh," Darrien said. He was not used to having a bunch of people overtly in his business. At least at his church, if people had questions or comments, they whispered behind his back. Shyanne's friends were bold. He figured it was because they were trying to protect their friend.

"Well, we were talking about our views on cheating and I got in my feelings and blew up. I was bogus for snapping at him because he had not done anything to me. I was just being paranoid," Shyanne admitted.

"So, you all just randomly were talking about cheating and you lost your marbles?" Selena asked. She knew somehow, some way, she and her business had come up in their conversation.

"She was explaining why cheating was a deal breaker for her," Darrien said.

"I don't blame you. Cheaters are so selfish. If you really loved someone you would honor them and not cheat," Kyra added.

"You know what? To me, it depends," Selena spoke up.

All of a sudden, the entire room got quiet, waiting eagerly to hear what Selena would say.

"Depends?" Cole said in disbelief.

"Yes. You know, cheating isn't about you, it's about the individual who can't keep it in their pants. They might love your dirty drawers, but loving you does not mean they love themselves. See, when you love yourself, you won't sabotage the best thing that has ever happened to you. No one in their right mind would kill love," Selena said.

"Man, that's deep," Rashawn said.

"I pray for cheaters. How do you think I've been able to go on since the whole scandal? I had to realize the fact that it's not that he did not love me. Kyle loved the ground I walked on. But Kyle did not love Kyle enough to protect the best thing that ever happened to him. He didn't love himself enough to believe he deserved my love—and he messed it up. This is not excusing cheating. I just want everyone to find someone who loves themselves enough to be faithful."

"That was heavy," Darrien said.

The entire mood had shifted in the party. They were not sad, but the room was much more serious than it had been just minutes earlier. Kyra decided she needed to break the ice.

"Ok, I have margaritas! Who wants one?"

"Me!"

"Alright, well I want to propose a toast," Lisa said. "I want to toast to new friendships, love, peace, and soul."

They all drank up and chatted more. Kyra looked around and noticed Lisa and Rashawn had been talking for a bit. Kyra got her attention then winked.

"So," Rashawn said.

"So, what?" Lisa asked with a smirk.

"You're gorgeous."

"Thank you. You're quite handsome yourself," Lisa replied.

"I guess we'll be seeing each other a lot since it looks like these cakes are really serious," Rashawn said referring to Darrien and Shyanne, who had not stopped giggling and flirting since they sat down.

"We probably will," Lisa said with a smile.

"Hmm... So, what is that scent you're wearing?"

"Um, it's called Sky Di Gioia by Giorgio Armani."

Rashawn leaned in and whispered in Lisa's ear, "You're not going to be able to wear that around me."

"And why is that?" Lisa asked none the wiser.

"Because it's an aphrodisiac and I'm trying to stay saved," he admitted.

"Oop," Lisa said and looked around to see if anyone could hear what he had said.

Selena was into her phone most of the time, but everyone had a great time. They did not even get a chance to watch the movie. They played Uno, Truth or Dare, and Mentally Stimulate Me. Everyone had a great time getting to know one another. The guests began to leave around 11:00 pm because everyone had to be at church in the morning. Shyanne kissed Darrien goodnight and stayed behind to help Kyra clean up.

"So," Shyanne struck up a conversation while they washed dishes, "what do you think about me and Darrien? I am in love with that man, Pud. He is literally the best."

"Well, honestly, he seems like a nice guy, but I am concerned about you guys moving at lightning speed. I want what's best for you and I just hope it all works out," Kyra said.

"I feel you. The timeline was scaring me, too, but I think God's hand is on it and we will work out."

227

"I feel you. Just do not lose yourself in him or anyone else. Make sure you stay focused on your dreams and your brand. You know you're a hopeless romantic." Kyra was jokingly serious. She thought Darrien was a cool guy, but she needed to know why everything was on turbo time with him? Why could they not slow down and figure each other out? Shyanne had confided in their circle that she and Darrien had been talking about getting married. They had only dated three months, and although they had known each other their whole lives, Kyra thought it was too fast. As the married one in the group, she knew that marriage rocked, but it was also as hard as rocks. She and Cole were a great couple and they loved each other very much, but there were times when both of them wanted to give up. However, the friendship that they had built lent them a solid foundation. Kyra just wanted her friend to have a foundation. But if Shyanne did not want to listen to her, there was nothing she could do about it.

Chapter 21

When Shyanne's alarm rang, she had no choice but to hit the snooze button on her phone. It was as if her index finger involuntarily moved on its own to touch the word "snooze". She was the personification of tired that day. After she got home from Kyra's house around one o'clock in the morning, she could not sleep. All she did was think about her potential future with Darrien the entire night.

Although she understood where her best friend Kyra was coming from, the truth was she and Darrien knew all they could possibly want to know about each other from dating. They knew each other's favorite colors, food, what styles of homes they liked, how many children they wanted to have, and what made each of them happy or angry. Shyanne knew that nothing aggravated Darrien more than hypocrites and the silent treatment. He was also a better communicator than she was. They were cut from the same cloth. The things that took others one year to learn, they learned in weeks. The timing was scary, but Shyanne had prayed, and she felt like this was God's doing; and it felt good.

Two snooze pushes later, Shyanne got up groggy and already ready to get back in her bed. She stepped over to her walk-in closet and picked out her clothes for the day. Because Shyanne was the chairperson, she decided to represent for the youth and make the uniform denim and white. Shyanne pulled out an oversized, distressed denim jacket that read "God is dope!" on the sleeves, front and back. She pulled out white denim jeggings she got from Ashley Stewart, a white v neck t-shirt, and rose gold pointy toe pumps. She wanted to look casual, but chic, so she grabbed a rose gold statement necklace that she'd purchased from Ms. Tish over at Dress Code boutique. And because she knew that at some point in the day she would be removing those pumps, she put a pair of metallic rose gold gym shoes into her purse.

Shyanne walked over to her bed and grabbed her phone. She noticed there was one message from Darrien.

Darrien:
Good morning, beautiful. I know you're probably getting ready for church. I'm not going to come to the morning service. I want to study a little bit more to make sure I'm ready for the evening service. I love you and can't wait to see you. -Bae

Shyanne's heart melted. She could not wait to see him later. She connected her phone to her bathroom's Bluetooth speakers, went to her music playlist and selected Jonathan McReynold's station. He was this dope gospel artist from Chicago with a soul vibe that she loved. The first song that came on from the playlist was his new song "Not Lucky, I'm Loved". Shyanne took that as a personal message from God. This love story brewing between her and Darrien was not a coincidence or by chance. It was not because of luck, but because of God's love.

Shyanne placed her shower cap on her head and got in the shower. She began to sing and thank God for always loving her. Although she woke up tired and groggy, in the pit of her gut, she felt like today was going to be a great day. She had worked really hard with the church, especially the youth, for the past four months to prepare for today. She was excited to see all of her efforts come together.

Once Shyanne got out of the shower, beat her face, and got dressed, she knocked on her guest bedroom door to see if Selena was getting ready for church. When she knocked, Selena did not answer the door. Shyanne walked down the stairs to see if she was down there and found her in the kitchen, eating a bagel, dressed and ready to go.

"Hey, girl," Shyanne said as she hugged her sister.

"Good morning. I ordered Uber Eats. Your bagel is in the microwave."

"Yum! You order the best food. What's on it?" Shyanne asked as she walked over to the microwave.

"It's a Lox. It has regular cream cheese, salmon, a little tomato, and capers. Well, I told them to take the tomatoes off yours."

"Aww," Shyanne motioned a heart with her hands, "you know me so well. So, what are you down here doing?"

"Honestly, I was thinking about finding a Christian counselor or therapist."

"For what?"

"Because I think I hate my former best friend and I want to forgive her. I do not want to befriend her, but I do want to let this go. I literally get sick thinking about her and I replay the events of how we found out every single day. I need answers, but I need to know how I can move on without getting the closure I need."

Shyanne felt so bad for her sister. Dealing with this level of trauma and continuing throughout life without addressing it could not possibly be healthy.

"Well, I'm here for it. Go ahead and do what you have to do, Sissy. I support you 100%."

They ate their food and headed right to the church. They went into their father's office to speak, and to their surprise, Bishop and Lady Roberts, Darrien's parents, were sitting in the office.

"Oh, good morning, Bishop. Good morning, First Lady. How are you two?" Shyanne asked.

"We're doing wonderful, sweetheart. We came up to support you and Darrien. I can't wait to hear my baby," Lady Roberts said.

"Uh, Darrien is not preaching until this evening, but we brought a few people from the church to have service with you all and your mother invited us to have dinner at your parents' house afterward. Are you going to come?" Bishop Darrien asked, putting Shyanne on the spot.

"Oh, I did not know that you all were going to have dinner with my parents today," she looked up at her Dad, "I wish I had. I would have gotten someone to fill in for me. We have one final rehearsal for the kids' dance after service."

"It's ok, darling," Lady Roberts said. "We will see you for the evening service."

"Selena how are you this morning?" Bishop Lawson asked.

"Good morning, Daddy. I'll be fine," she offered him a smile. "Well, we better get out here, so we can march in with the choir.

"Alright, see you all in a bit."

Morning service was awesome. Selena and Shyanne's baby sister Skylar even gave the inspirational message. Shyanne's family could not have been prouder.

In between services, Shyanne stayed at the church to help the dancers rehearse their dance moves for the umpteenth time. The girls were dancing to "Lord Make Me Whole" by Ron Poindexter. The song was pretty powerful so the girls were nervous, but Shyanne was there to reassure them that they'd be fine.

Meanwhile, in Naperville at the Lawson house, there was a light dinner party. Unbeknownst to Shyanne, Darrien was over her parents' house with his parents, the Lawson children, Rashawn, Marvin, Tim, and Lisa. Kyra could not attend because she had church duties, but she would be at service that evening. Bishop Lawson had personally invited everyone to service that evening because instead of it being the Family and Friend's Day service Shyanne had planned, their church was surprising Shyanne with an Appreciation Service to recognize all of the hard work she put into the ministry. Everyone was in on it but Shyanne. They were all so excited. The Lawsons had ordered some pans of chicken, biscuits, mashed potatoes, corn and biscuits for everyone to feast on and hang out until the second service.

"Hey, Bishop Lawson, may I speak with you and the Missus in private for a moment?" Darrien asked.

"Sure, son. Just go into the kitchen, we'll be right behind you."

Darrien walked into the kitchen and moments later, the Lawsons followed behind him.

"What can I help you with, son?" Bishop Lawson asked.

"Well, I would just like to thank you for allowing me to date your daughter, sir. I followed your guidelines and I feel like she is someone very special."

"Is that right?" Bishop Lawson said. He glanced at his wife and shifted his stance.

"Sir," he paused to collect himself, "I really feel like your daughter is the person I want to be with for the rest of my life. I prayed and asked God, and all I see is Shyanne. I love you and I love you, Lady Eva, like my second parents. And I wanted to talk to you today to ask your blessing to ask your daughter for her hand in marriage."

Lady Eva's eyes bucked as she heard the news. She did not want to speak out of turn, she wanted her husband to say something first. She looked to her left and saw her husband had begun to pace the floor.

"Son, are you sure you're ready to get married? That is a life-long commitment."

"I'm sure. She is my missing rib," Darrien said as he stood firm.

"Now, son, you know we just dealt with one child over here getting her heartbroken, we do not need a repeat—you understand?" Bishop asked.

"I understand fully, sir."

"Good, because she might be your rib, but if you break her heart, I'm going to break you and repent later," Bishop Lawson said as he eyed Darrien.

"I will not break her heart, sir."

"Ok. If she says yes, you have my blessing. You're a fine young man."

"Thank you, sir," Darrien said as he began to smile from ear to ear.

Lady Eva jumped up and down and said, "You can officially call me 'Ma!'"

They all hugged and were excited about the impending proposal.

"Come on, put those hands together!" Shyanne encouraged as she led the congregation in worship. Everyone was up on their feet singing the call and response song.

"Great is the Lord!" Shyanne and the audience sang over and over. She jumped up and down and sang the song to the top of her lungs. She really began to feel what she was singing. God had truly been great to her. She was only twenty-five years old, she owned her own business, made six figures, had a great family and great friends. Although she had some downs in her life, including her relationship with her mom, her friendship ending with Miriam, and feeling overwhelmed by life, she was doing well. As Shyanne sang, she glanced to her right. The look on Darrien and her father's faces solidified it for her—life was great, God is great.

Darrien looked at Shyanne with a look of admiration, love, and relief. Darrien had dealt with his fair share of women in the past, but none compared to Shyanne. His heart felt safe in her hands. Besides, right now, she was looking more beautiful than ever. Her long, natural hair was in a wild, curly twist out. Her curls bounced as she sang. More than aesthetically, Darrien thought she was most beautiful when she worshipped God.

The band followed Shyanne to a 't.' Praise & Worship was amazing. When Shyanne turned the mic over to her father, she was still filled with excitement about the greatness of God.

"You may be seated in the presence of the Lord," Bishop Lawson said. "Today is Family and Friend's Day and our committee has prepared a great service for tonight. Please, give our committee a round of applause. And let's give God glory for Sis. Shyanne Lawson for being the chairperson and putting this wonderful service together."

As the people applauded, Shyanne cringed. She did not know how to accept the outpouring of love and admiration from so many people; she felt very awkward.

"Now, I know Shyanne had an awesome service planned for today, but things are going to go a little bit differently. Shyanne, can you join me up here?"

Shyanne gave her father the side eye and came forward. She said an inward prayer, hoping he would not embarrass her in front of Darrien and all of the attendees.

"Shyanne, instead of having Family and Friend's Day service, our church is dedicating this service to you. This is your appreciation service. Thank you for all of your hard work and dedication to the youth and to this church."

Suddenly, the house lights went out, the spotlights came on and the dancers came out and danced to "Anthem of Praise". Shyanne was so surprised, she began to cry. She laid her head on her dad's shoulder and cried. She felt so overwhelmed by love and support.

After the dancers danced, the choir sang. After the choir, each dancer Shyanne worked with from the youth department came over to the mic, said something about Shyanne and gave her a balloon.

"Ms. Shyanne said I can be what I want to be; I love her, and she is my best friend," eight-year-old Trinity said.

"I love you, Ms. Shyanne," twelve-year-old Joshua said nervously.

The parents came up and thanked her for being such a great example to their children, and then all a sudden, the Lawson children were on the stage. They all had great words to say. First, Skylar came up and talked about how much she admired her sister. After Skylar, Steven, Jr., expressed how much he looked up to his big sister and he also expressed how he hoped she would leave him her boutique in her will. Shyanne was so embarrassed.

Then, Selena took the mic with tears in her eyes. "Sister, it has always been my job to protect you. I was raised to beat people up for you," she quipped. "I am proud of the woman you have become. Thank you for always having my back. I'm with you until the wheels fall off."

"And so am I!" Kyra and Lisa came from backstage and joined everyone else. "Thank you for being my Best."

"We love you for real," Lisa added.

"Oh my God!" Shyanne said. She was now bawling.

The audience began to clap and cheer as Lady Lawson joined her husband and family on the stage. "Shyanne. No matter what, I love you for real. I am your biggest cheerleader. You're going to be amazing."

Shyanne looked over her right shoulder and saw Darrien. She began to put two and two together and started jumping up and down.

"Well, Baby Girl," Bishop Lawson said, "I've raised you from a kitten to a tomcat, and I can say, I could not be prouder of the woman you have become. You know church, the Bible tells us to train them up, and my baby did not depart. It has been my great pleasure to be your father, your protector, your pastor, and it is even a greater pleasure for me to pass the baton. Everybody stand to your feet with me as we give God glory for the Assistant Pastor of the Freedom Temple Church of Carbondale, Pastor Darrien Roberts."

There was not a dry eye in the building. The band began to play "Perfect Love Song" by Anita Wilson to set the mood.

"Shyanne, I was reading the scriptures about this woman in Proverbs the thirty-first chapter. And my God if it wasn't you. Shyanne, you have the innocence of Eve, the strength of Abigail, the prayers of Sarah, the faith of Ruth, the ministry of Priscilla, the bravery of Esther, the wisdom of Deborah, you hold me down like Zipporah, and you're holy like Mary."

Everybody cheered.

"I want to do life with you because I can't see it without you. Let's be fruitful and multiply, girl."

The crowd began to laugh at his Biblical joke, including Shyanne.

"Shyanne Janelle Lawson," he got down on one knee. "Will you marry me?"

Shyanne cried and jumped up and down. "Absolutely!" Darrien placed a beautiful, Tiffany & Co. ring on her ring finger. Shyanne was in awe of the solitaire diamond. It was exactly what she wanted.

The entire church got up and cheered. Shyanne was getting ready to change her last name. Everyone took photos of the platinum ring and the happy couple. Nothing could ruin this moment.

Chapter 22

Ms. Black looked at her daughter with sorrow in her eyes. It was difficult to see your child going through something and not be able to kiss the boo-boo and make it all better. Although her baby was a grown woman, she had still gone through a world of trouble and here she was in her home, all alone. When Ms. Black heard that her daughter, Miriam, was in the hospital, she dropped everything and came to see her. Ms. Black was shocked to find Kyle asleep in the chair next to her bed. She had only known Kyle as Miriam's best friend's boyfriend. She had seen him out and about at different events, but she did not know he had a rapport with her daughter, let alone one close enough for him to be in her hospital room.

She eyed her daughter, who was asleep and hooked up to several machines. When the nurse called her, she was told that Miriam had experienced some trauma and she was stable. She had also been told that Miriam's blood pressure had been extremely high, and they had kept her overnight to observe her progress. Ms. Black had gotten there as soon as she could and now she needed answers.

She woke Kyle up and asked what he was doing there. He had a pained look on his face and told her that Miriam would need to explain the situation when she woke up.

When Kyle saw that her mother was going to stay with Miriam, he left. He was only there because he thought she did not have anyone else. He had been trying his best to shake this woman since the day of their first indiscretion—he was never successful. This time, he would be. He needed to get rid of her. The bad thing was that they had lost a baby in the process of their foolishness.

Kyle could not believe himself. He had gone from knowing he wanted to spend the rest of his life with Selena to all of that being taken away from him with one lapse of judgment…well, a few lapses. He had to go away and get himself together. He needed to do some serious reflecting to know why he messed up his for sure stuff for some more stuff.

Ms. Black asked her daughter what had happened, and to her surprise, Miriam told the truth. Ms. Black had seen the viral video of Selena fighting but she had no idea the one receiving the punches and kicks was her child. She could not even be upset. If her best friend had betrayed her the way Miriam had betrayed Selena, she knew she would be in prison right now. She was completely disgusted by her daughter's actions. She had not raised her to be a whore. She was even more astonished when Miriam told her that she had lost her job. How could Ms. Black not know what was going on with her only child? She was her grown child, but her child nevertheless. It pained her to know that she did not feel comfortable enough to ask her mother for help.

A month later, Ms. Black watched her daughter sit on her couch and scroll her life away on her phone. There was no denying that her baby was depressed. She had not spoken much since she left the hospital. Ms. Black had gone to Miriam's apartment, packed her things and moved her back home. She put Miriam on a payment plan for all of her bills and decided to help her daughter rebuild. Truthfully, she did not recognize her child anymore. She was in love with someone else's man. The way she pined over Kyle and the memories of Kyle was disheartening, to say the least. This version of Miriam was without couth and egregious. But Ms. Black still loved her, and she had to be there for her because no one else was. Miriam had screwed her friends away.

"Mama," Miriam said just above a whisper.

"Yes, baby?"

"Have you been on Facebook today?"

"I have. Why do you ask?"

"Did you see all of these pictures? Shyanne is getting married to Darrien," Miriam said slowly.

"I saw them. Are you ok?"

"No," Miriam cried, and her chest heaved up and down. "I hate this. I wish I could congratulate this girl. I can't even speak to her."

Ms. Black came over and rubbed her back. "Well, you know what they say, 'time heals all wounds.' Maybe one day, you all will work it out." Ms. Black did not even believe what she was saying. She just wanted to make her feel good.

"And then look at Selena smiling in all of these pictures. I should have pressed charges on her. How does she get to kill my baby and still roam free like it's nothing?" Miriam said. Her lip curled at the memory of her fatal fight with her former best friend.

"Miriam, you have to remember, she did not just fight you for no reason. You cannot upset yourself like that. You have to pray and try to move forward."

Miriam did not even respond to her mother, she just kept scrolling on Facebook. Shyanne had a smile plastered across her face and Selena was right with her. Kyra and Lisa were all there too, but no one was with her. She was all by herself and no one cared. She did thank God for the time she had spent with Kyle though. She vowed that she would get her family back. She and Kyle were a family. They had a bond. Although their baby, Khy, had passed, she was still theirs. She could give him another baby or anything he wanted. All she needed was him.

Miriam scrolled and spotted a photo of Selena lifting Shyanne's ring finger. "It's ok, I'm going to get you for Khy," she vowed allowed.

Ms. Black heard her daughter say something, but she was not sure what she was talking about or whom she was talking to. *Who is Khy?* She thought to herself. It was not lost upon her that her baby seemed to be in another world. It was almost as if she were possessed.

When she tried to look Miriam in the eye, Miriam's eyes could never quite connect with her—she had an aloof look in her eye. Miriam rarely spoke, and when she did, it was barely audible. Ms. Black originally thought the cause of her issues was stemming from one of the medications she had been on for her blood pressure, but now, she was second-guessing herself. She did not know what the issue really was. She had a few hypotheses; but regardless of the cause, Ms. Black just wanted her daughter back.

"Miriam, I've been thinking. With the loss of your baby and your friends, you've been through a lot in the last month or so. What do you think about going to see a counselor? They can help you sort out your feelings and maybe make you feel better."

Miriam was silent. She knew her mother was only trying to help, but it felt like she was just calling her crazy. It did not matter what her mother thought. It did not matter what Kyle thought. It did not matter who else had thoughts about her situation. None of the people with opinions were there in the fetal position as a baby was beaten out of them.

"I don't know, Mom. I just want to go to bed. I have a headache."

Miriam got up and went to her room. She was trying to think of ways to get revenge on Selena. When she could not think of anything, she just cried herself to sleep.

Ms. Black sat at her living room table in disbelief. She wished Miriam would feel better. She said a silent prayer for strength while dealing with this entire ordeal. Miriam had only been staying with her for a month and she was stressed out—it was even starting to show on her face. She had wrinkles from worrying plastered across her forehead. Ms. Black knew she had to keep herself calm before she ended up in the hospital herself. It was easier said than done.

Chapter 23

"Thank you, guys, for spending the night with me. I needed you guys here," Shyanne said to Kyra, Selena and Lisa.

"You better never, ever say I don't love you. Am I taking time away from my whole husband to spend the night over here? Tuh!" Kyra playfully teased her friend.

"You better know I know you love me. So, how long did you guys know he was going to propose?" Shyanne asked.

"Well, Kyra and I found out yesterday; but Selena has known for the longest," Lisa said.

"Yes, I've known for a couple of weeks. I helped my brother pick out the ring. We did good, right?" Selena asked.

"Yes, you guys did so well. Thank you." Shyanne replied.

"Baby, you ready to be a First Lady?" Lisa asked.

"Well, technically, his mother is the First Lady of his church, but I am ready to be his wife. His wife? Y'all, I am engaged in real life!" She exclaimed.

"Yes, you are!" Kyra jumped up and down with her friend.

Shyanne had invited her friends to spend the night to celebrate her engagement. She was in a state of astonishment. Everything seemed to feel so surreal, like a dream—a dream come true. She prayed to thank God for this moment, one she had longed for forever.

"So, let me ask you this. Why are you spending your engagement night with us instead of with your man? 'Cause I would not be with any of you heifers if a man proposed to me," Lisa jested.

"Truth be told, it's because I'm trying to wait until marriage to have sex, and he has never been more sexy to me than he was the moment he got down on his knee and proposed. I needed to make sure I did not invite him to my house; thus, you're here," Shyanne said flat out.

"That's the realest thing you have ever said. That engagement period is the most tempting time of all. Your mind will tell you, 'well, you're going to get married anyway; so, technically, he is your husband.' Baby, it's hard not to fall into temptation before you hit that altar," Kyra said from experience.

"For real, Best. People act like abstinence is a walk in the park. It is not. But the thing that keeps us is, we honor our vows to God more than we desire each other. So, we're waiting to do this thing. Oh, but in that great getting up morning." Shyanne got up and pretended to shout like she was in church. Her friends got up and joined her, humming the music for their praise break.

Shyanne could not be happier that she had three friends who she could count on, love and trust with her entire heart. When they all came down from their pseudo praise break, they laughed and giggled; but Shyanne was thinking about Miriam. This was the kind of moment they would normally share with her. It was weird not having Miriam around. How could one go from speaking to a person every single day to never hearing from them again? Shyanne hated what she did; however, she did feel the weight of the missing link to their circle.

"You know, it's weird not having Miriam here," Shyanne said. Her eyes darted directly to Selena who had a blank expression on her face.

"It is. But I'm not trying to have her around me. She is a snake," Selena said with fierceness.

"I get that. And I do not want her around me either because we cannot trust her; but if she were to totally get it together, apologize for real and change, would you accept it?" Kyra wanted to know.

"I was going to ask you that, too," Lisa chimed in.

"Look, I would prefer that we stopped talking about this girl altogether. It has not been that long since this happened. I can tell you right now that we will never be friends again; so, please, stop bringing up this bald-headed girl to me. Ok?"

"Ok," Shyanne, Lisa, and Kyra said in unison.

Their intention was not to upset Selena, but Miriam was a touchy subject. Shyanne wanted to know if her sister would ever get the apology she deserved from Kyle and Miriam.

"Well, on another note, Lisa and I are going to Carbondale Tuesday. I'm so excited," Shyanne tried to lighten the mood.

"When is Darrien going back?" Lisa asked.

"He's going back tomorrow. Selena and I have to do inventory at Pizazz; so, we're going to go after them."

"Girl, Lady Roberts is going to give you a crash course in First Lady-hood 101," Kyra teased.

"I already know, she's going to be like 'can you cook? Cause my baby likes to eat.' Girl, the lady is about to drill me!"

All the girls laughed and kept on laughing on into the night. Once again, life was changing; the circle was shifting.

Darrien grabbed his duffle bag and was heading to the front desk to check out of his hotel room. It was a beautiful day outside. The sun was shining brightly. The chilly winds were still blowing, but there was no doubt that Spring had arrived. Darrien adjusted his duffle bag on his right shoulder and headed to the elevator.

He and his family were heading back home to Carbondale. He came to Chicago single and was leaving out engaged. He was about to marry the sunshine of his life. He celebrated his engagement with his friends closest to him – Rashawn, Marvin, and Tim. They stayed up and talked the entire night. Darrien wondered what Shyanne and her friends were doing, but he bet they were doing much of the same.

After Darrien checked out of the hotel, he saw Rashawn pull his SUV in front of the hotel. Before he got into that car, he walked over to the car his mother and father were in.

"Pop," he shook his father's hand and leaned into his father's window. "Thank you for coming and holding the secret, man."

"I love you, son. You've done well for yourself. A young man, you got your own business, and you love the Lord with all your heart. I could not be prouder of you," Bishop Roberts said.

"Thank you, Pop." Darrien lived for his father's approval. His father was his biggest influence, toughest critic, and role model. If Bishop Darrien Roberts, Sr. said it, it was gold.

"Yes, baby. We are so proud of you, Choc," Lady Roberts said. She was the only one in their family who still called Darrien by his childhood nickname.

Darrien walked to the passenger's side to kiss his mother on the cheek.

"Thank you, Mama. I love you."

"Alright, son. Are you guys trailing behind us?" Bishop Roberts asked.

"Yeah, we are. When we get near downtown Chicago, I'm going to drop off and head to Shyanne's boutique to say bye to her, then catch back up to you guys."

"Alright, son. Love you, man."

"Love you, too." Darrien turned away to leave.

"Wait, D.J." Darrien's mom called out. He came back around to her side of the vehicle.

"Yes, ma'am?"

"I forgot to ask you if you had any aspirin or pain meds. I forgot to buy some at the hotel, and your Dad's arm has been bothering him. I think he slept on it wrong or something," Lady Roberts asked.

"Cheryl, you did not have to worry that boy. When we stop at the gas station, I'm going to get some aspirin and I will be fine," Bishop Roberts said agitated.

"Are you sure, Pop? I have some packed in my bag. I could go and get it really quickly."

"I'm sure. Go 'head and get in the car so we can hit the road before the rush hour."

Darrien jogged back to the car. Rashawn opened the door to let him in. Darrien immediately pulled his phone out of his pocket and texted Shyanne to let her know he would be at Pizazz in thirty minutes. She sent him back a kissy face emoji. Darrien was having a great day. He was slightly concerned about his father though. Bishop Roberts was not the type to complain. If he was feeling pained, he would just ride it out; but the fact that he said something to Lady Roberts made him feel like it was excruciating. Darrien closed his eyes and prayed that his father would feel better.

Darrien drifted off to sleep and woke up to the sound of Rashawn calling his name. "Pastor. Pastor Roberts. Darrien!"

Darrien's eyes popped open and he tried to adjust his eyesight. He looked at Rashawn and said, "Where are we?"

"We're at your girl's store. Wake up, man." Rashawn walked around to Darrien's door and opened it.

"Thanks, man." Darrien yawned, stretched, adjusted his clothes and hopped out of the car. He walked into the boutique and immediately spotted Shyanne helping a customer. She smiled at him and kept helping her customer.

Darrien chuckled to himself because of Shyanne's presentation. She had on an oversized blue button up shirt with some distressed jeans and black, peep-toe booties. She looked very pretty with her hair pulled up in a high ponytail and no makeup. Her appearance was not what humored him, it was her gestures. He'd known Shyanne practically his entire life, but he had never seen her talk with her hands so much. Shyanne was subconsciously flashing her engagement ring every three seconds.

Once she was done talking to the customer, she walked over to him.

"Say, sir, you're over here looking kind of fine. You got a woman at home?"

"Naw, I do not. But you're pretty cute. I would like to wife you if you're going," he played along.

"Well, my future husband might beat you up, but I'd risk it all for a handsome man like you," Shyanne leaned in and kissed Darrien fully on the lips.

"Wow," Darrien responded. "Well, I was just coming to say see you later and I love you."

"I love you, too, baby. I'll see you tomorrow. Lisa and I are leaving at six in the morning, so I should get there around noon, give or take a few minutes," Shyanne said.

"Ok," he walked towards the door. "Shyanne."

"Yes?"

"I told you we would get married one day, didn't I?" He asked, recalling their initial phone conversation.

"You sure did," she laughed.

"You know you have my heart, right?" Darrien asked.

"I know," Shyanne flashed her ring and smiled.

"See you tomorrow."

Darrien ran in the cool air to get back in the car. He was so tired that within minutes, he had fallen asleep.

Four hours into their car ride, Darrien was awakened by an ear-splitting scream. He jumped up out of his sleep to see Rashawn, Marvin, and Tim looking startled and concerned. Darrien's eyes shifted around the vehicle. Everything looked ok. He looked outside, and everything looked normal. He had to have been dreaming. Darrien was visibly shaken.

"Aye, D.J.," Marvin said. "Are you alright, man?"

"Y'all didn't hear that?" Darrien said as he adjusted his posture.

"We didn't hear anything. What's going on?" Rashawn asked from behind the wheel.

"It's like I heard someone do a real, high-pitched scream. It really scared me," Darrien admitted.

"Man, you were dreaming, dude," Tim said, "go back to sleep."

But Darrien would not be able to sleep right away after that. He was wide awake. They had two more hours to go on the ride home.

One hour later, Darrien had started to drift off to sleep, then he felt the vibration of his phone ringing. Without looking, Darrien answered.

"Hello?"

All Darrien could hear in his ear was screams. This time, he knew it was not a dream or a drill; this was happening in real life. He looked down at his phone in a panic. It was his mother. He put the phone on speaker and tried to remain calm.

"Ma, ma, stop screaming and tell me what's wrong," he said in a shaky but calm voice.

"Your father!" His mother cried hysterically.

"Aye, what's going on, D?" Marvin asked.

Darrien ignored him and focused on his mother.

"Mom breathe so you can tell me what's wrong. I cannot fix it if you do not tell me what's going on," Darrien spoke.

Lady Roberts took a deep breath and said, "I'm in an ambulance with your father, we're already in Carbondale heading to the hospital." She began to cry again.

"Ma, please stop crying so I can hear you. Why is Pop in an ambulance?"

"You know he has been talking about his arm. We were on our way here and your Dad started to pull over to the side of the road right when we were going to exit. He told me to call 911 and I did and then I looked over and he was just slumped over, and we had hit the wall! I think he had a heart attack! Baby, I can't breathe. Pray. Pray for your father! I cannot do life without him!" Lady Roberts' chest and shoulders heaved up and down as she cried hysterically. "Darrien, Sr., you're going to pull through, baby! I'm right here. I'm not gon' let nothing take you from us. It ain't your time. You gon' live and not die! I got enough faith to pull you through, baby."

"Ma'am, we're going to take him in now." Darrien heard the paramedics say.

"Ma, I'm on my way to the hospital now. He's going to make it," Darrien said but he was not really sure.

"Yes, he is. He has no choice. Hurry up and get here. I need you to hold your mama up." She said and hung up.

Darrien closed his eyes. Here he was asleep while his hero was in distress. Darrien felt so helpless and alone.

"D.J., we'll get you to the hospital, but your Dad is going to be ok, man. Let's pray," Marvin said. He turned to look into the back seat where Darrien was sitting and grabbed his hand; Tim, who was sitting in the back seat with Darrien, took his left hand and touched Rashawn's shoulder.

"Father, we thank You for being God. We pray right now, in Your name, that You would keep the Bishop, Lord. You have all power in Your most capable hands. I pray that You will shield and bless Lady Roberts and Pastor Darrien and give them strength to deal with this. We believe you now for Bishop's complete and total healing. It's in Jesus' name, amen."

Darrien began to cry aloud. He believed God, but this was a tough pill to swallow. His dad was in distress. He had to cry his eyes out before he got to the hospital because he had to be his mother's strength. When the tears stopped flowing, he decided to call Shyanne—he could not handle this alone.

Shyanne answered the phone on the first ring. "Hey, babe!"

"I need you."

Chapter 24

Shyanne and Lisa got to Carbondale in a record-breaking five hours after she had received the phone call from her fiancé. She was distraught, but she kept a good poker face for her future husband. She had already called her father and told him what was happening. Bishop and Lady Lawson would arrive in Carbondale the next day. Selena stayed back in Chicago, so she could run Pizazz. She and Kyra definitely sent their prayers up for Bishop Roberts. Everyone believed God that he would come through.

Lisa pulled up in front of the hospital and let Shyanne out as she went to park. Shyanne stopped at the front desk.

"Who you here to see?" the receptionist asked. She was barely paying attention to her job. She was wearing a uniform that was about two sizes too small, a nose ring, and long, multicolored weave. The dye from her hair was bleeding onto her white shirt. Shawty looked a mess and acted one, too. She just picked at her nails and scrolled down Instagram on her phone.

"Um, firstly, hello. And I'm here to see Bishop Darrien Roberts, Sr."

"Well, do you know what unit he's in?" The Trap Receptionist asked, with plenty of attitude.

"Are you ok?" Shyanne asked, not in the mood for this woman's poor attitude.

"I'm good and you?"

"Great. Now, if you could look him up on your computer, I could go and see Bishop Darrien Roberts."

"You ain't gotta do all that. I just asked you do you know what unit he in." The Trap Receptionist began to search for Bishop Robert's name in the system. "Take the East elevator to floor number three. He is in room 309. It's a long walk so be careful. You might trip," she shot at Shyanne.

"Baby, you better hope I don't or I will sue this hospital and rename it Roberts Medical; and guess who will be in the unemployment office? Oh, no. Cat got your tongue? You better be careful who you talk crazy to because I'm not the one or the two!"

Shyanne snatched her visitor's pass from off the desk and strutted to the east elevator, leaving the trash at the desk eating her dust. She swiftly got on the elevator and pressed the number 3. "Ok, Jesus. Please, do not let us lose Bishop Roberts. At least not while Darrien is so excited about getting married. It's a whole lot to deal with. Please, give him a miracle."

Just as she finished her prayer, the elevator doors opened. She walked what seemed like a country mile to get to Bishop Roberts' room. As soon as she got there, security was at the door.

"Are you family?" The security guard said.

"Yes, I'm his daughter."

"Do you have an ID?"

"Let my fiancé through the door," she heard Darrien say on the opposite side of the door.

"Oh, man. We didn't know this was you. Come on in, sweetheart."

"Thank you," Shyanne said, "there's a young lady named Lisa who is coming up here in about five minutes. She had to park the car. She is family, too."

"Yes, ma'am," the security said as he held the door for her to walk in.

Shyanne immediately threw her arms around Darrien's neck. His eyes were so puffy and tired. It was clear he had been crying. He broke their embrace and just looked at Shyanne through teary eyes. Shyanne used her thumbs to wipe his tears away.

"I'm here, ok?" Shyanne said. "I'm not leaving your side. Let me go over here and speak to your mom."

"She's asleep. Let's go in the family waiting area," Darrien suggested. He took his hand in hers and led her around the corner to the waiting room. The only people in there were Rashawn, Marvin, and Tim.

"Hey, brothers," Shyanne hugged and greeted them.

"Hey, Shy," Marvin said.

"What's up, Lil Sis?" Tim greeted.

"We weren't expecting you here until tomorrow. It's great to see you," Rashawn acknowledged.

"Well, you know I'm not going to leave my man alone. I came running. Speaking of..." Shyanne nodded her head towards the left. Rashawn turned and saw Lisa walking briskly down the hallway.

"I'm going to hit you back, sis," he said to Shyanne and walked over to Lisa.

"Babe, what's going on. Is your dad going to be ok?" Shyanne rubbed his back and asked genuinely.

"They're still running tests on him. My mother thought he had a heart attack, but he definitely had a mild stroke and his blood pressure is high. They've put him on blood thinners to prevent any more strokes. He's going to make it, but he will be in here for a while," Darrien said.

"Well, it's good to hear he is going to make it, and you will, too," Shyanne said as she stepped in for a hug.

"Shy, this is hard, man. He's always been my strength. It's so hard to see my Pop look so helpless. Man, I don't wish this on nobody."

"I know, but just think about the fact that he is going to be fine. It could have gone another way. Now, have you made any calls? Is there anyone who needs to be notified?" Shyanne asked.

"I want to make an official statement on the church's website and social media pages, but I need to make it clear that he is not receiving visitors at this time. And if family members want to come up here, can you screen them for me? I just can't do it right now," Darrien asked.

"Sure, babe. Whatever you need. I brought you, the guys, and your mom some food, too. I cooked before I left; so, I'll find out where the microwave is and heat it up for you guys; ok?"

"Ok."

Shyanne began to walk off.

"Shyanne," Darrien called out.

"Yes?" She twirled on her toes to face him.

"Thank you."

She winked at him and went to find the microwave. She warmed up the food she had brought and bought some drinks from the vending machine. Shyanne, Darrien, Marvin, Tim, Rashawn, Lady Roberts, and Lisa all sat in the waiting room feasting on baked chicken, sweet potatoes and baked macaroni and cheese. Shyanne had originally cooked the food before hearing about the stroke to impress her future mother in law. She did not know it would become comfort food.

As they ate, one of the guards came and informed Lady Roberts that her husband had awakened. After about seven minutes of being alone with her husband, she went to the waiting room to get Darrien and Shyanne. Shyanne held Darrien's hand tight, so he knew he was not by himself.

"Son," Bishop Roberts spoke in a low, raspy tone. He lifted his right hand for Darrien to shake. What a difference a few hours make. Bishop Roberts had just been vibrant and cracking jokes earlier, and now he was so vulnerable.

"Pop. You're pulling through, man," Darrien said as he held back tears.

"Man, with God, all things are possible. Hey, daughter," he said referring to Shyanne.

"Hey, Bishop," she said as she kissed him on the cheek.

"Man, do not ever let stress overtake you. I'm telling you kids what I know. Stress can kill you," Bishop said through tear-filled eyes. "I just thank God for another chance, children. So, if you ever see me and I'm not praising, slap me because I must have forgotten. I've got a reason."

"Yeah, Pop, you're a blessed man," Darrien agreed as he let the tears fall.

"Yes, sir, you are." Shyanne was starting to get misty as well.

"Well, Roberts, we talked about you retiring in the next two years—maybe the time is now," Lady Roberts spoke up.

"Retiring?" Darrien said.

"Yes, son. I want to just enjoy the fruits of my labor and preach on occasion. I've been grooming you for the past six months, giving you more responsibilities, letting you sit in more meetings—it is all because I want to step down, and I want you to take my place."

Darrien stood there in shock. He had no idea his father had been planning on retiring. It was an honor that his father wanted him to take over the ministry, but Darrien was not ready to run an entire church right now. He was just about to get settled and here comes life shaking the table. He looked over at Shyanne who had a look of bewilderment on her face. This was not only his life turning upside down, but hers, too. She had just agreed to do life with this man, and before she could even get down the aisle, she was thrust into being the First Lady. This was not what she had in mind.

"Dad, this is a lot to take in at once," Darrien said.

"I know son, but I believe you can do it," he said. Bishop Roberts' voice sounded so weak and frail. "Look at me son. I need you."

A tear ran down Bishop Roberts' face. He had to retire from ministry. He was stressed out. Bishop Roberts was a business owner, clergyman, family man, and everyone else's rock. Bishop Lawson was the only person he could discuss these feelings with.

Bishop Lawson could relate wholeheartedly. He had the same kinds of stresses in his life; he just dealt with it differently. Bishop Lawson refused to let other people's problems stress him out. Experience had taught him better than that. He worked out daily, prayed daily, and he knew how to turn his phone off and tune people out. Bishop Roberts, however, wore other people's issues like a second layer of skin. He was the one everyone came to when they had troubles and he would solve them. Being everyone else's problem solver had brought him to this place. He never took time for himself. He made a vow to God that he would no longer neglect himself or his wife, and from this point forward, they would be his first concern.

Lady Roberts often times felt neglected or like she came second to the quote-unquote people of God, but she just shook her head and kept it moving. Sometimes, she would go into the bathroom to cry as she looked at her stressed husband. She prayed for him more than she prayed for herself. Her husband was the one everyone came to when they needed a bill paid, advice, a job, or even attention. In Lady Roberts' eyes, she had never come in second place in her husband's heart; she was third—God first, the church second, and then her. So, when Bishop Roberts came to her saying he had been thinking about retiring, she was overjoyed. She would finally be able to get her husband to herself. She knew Darrien was most capable of leading the church and leading a life of balance. He had already proven that he could. He was an excellent speaker, business owner, and son; and because Shyanne was a Bishop's daughter, she knew how to stand by his side. In Lady Roberts' mind, it was the perfect scenario.

"Anything you need, Pop. I got you," Darrien said as he released Shyanne's hand, leaned down and hugged his father.

Shyanne was astounded. Although she both appreciated and admired the love, respect, and loyalty Darrien had for his father and to God, she wished that he would consult her before making a huge decision that would not only affect her life but his as well. She made a mental note to speak to him about it later. She could not sweep this under the rug because if she did, this would be a recurring motif in their lives. For now, she would just go along with it.

"Ok; I'll get everything going so we can inform the board. Darrien, you're going to do a great job and so are you, Shyanne," Lady Roberts boasted.

"Yay," Shyanne sarcastically shot under her breath.

The next morning, Shyanne sat in the waiting room asleep with a blanket draped over her shoulders. Darrien had asked if she wanted him to get her a hotel room, or perhaps if she wanted to stay at his parents' house, but Shyanne vehemently disagreed. She would not leave the hospital until Bishop Roberts did, no matter how tired she was.

Shyanne was so grateful to have her parents by her side. They had arrived around seven o'clock in the morning. Darrien was grateful to have them, too. He had not made a statement to the public about his father's health yet because he did not need the excess drama, but the support of family was all he needed.

Darrien thanked God every day for the gift He had given him that was in the person of Shyanne Janelle Lawson. She had not left his side, not once. She made sure he ate every day, even when he did not want to. She would go to the cafeteria and come back with food for everyone. She helped him to call and check on his barbershop while taking care of her own business, Pizazz. He could never take her for granted. She was one of a kind.

Shyanne was startled out of her sleep by the clicking sounds of several pairs of heeled shoes walking past. Shyanne opened her eyes and looked to her left. Darrien was no longer asleep by her side, and she saw what looked like ten people walk into Bishop Roberts' hospital room. Security was letting them in, so they must have been important. Shyanne looked around and the only people who were still in the waiting room were her, Lisa, who was still asleep, Rashawn, Marvin, and Tim. Even her parents were gone.

"Good morning, guys," Shyanne said. She used her hand to shield her morning breath.

"Good morning," all three guys said.

"Um, where are my parents and Darrien?"

"They're in the Bishop's room with the church's board members," Marvin informed.

Oh wow. They don't waste any time, do they? Shyanne thought to herself. It was official—this was actually happening. Shyanne got up, grabbed her purse and carry-on bag and headed to the washroom. She proceeded to do a bird bath in the sink, brush her teeth, and pull her natural hair up into a top knot. She put on a houndstooth print maxi dress and kept on the hospital socks a nurse had given her. Although they did not work with her outfit, she was comfortable.

By the time Shyanne went back to the waiting room, Darrien had walked out of Bishop Roberts' room to greet her.

"Good morning, beautiful," he said and offered her a peck on the lips.

"Morning. Did you want me to go and get you something? Is everything ok in there?" Shyanne asked.

"Yeah, um. We have a slight dilemma," Darrien said, and he looked down.

"Wait. What's going on? Darrien just tell me. I can handle it."

"Let's go in Dad's room and talk to the elders."

"Ok," Shyanne said. She was thoroughly confused as to what was going on.

"Good morning, sweetheart," her father said, greeting her with a hug.

"Good morning, Daddy. Good morning everybody. How are we feeling today, Bishop?" Shyanne said, as she gazed down at his face. Instead of seeing his usual cocoa colored skin, he looked grey and ashy. She was alarmed but tried her best not to showcase her concern on her face.

"I'm doing alright, daughter. I'm yet holding on," Bishop Roberts said in a hoarse voice.

274

"Ok. Allow me to fill in my soon-to-be daughter in love. As you know, Bishop Roberts is going to retire from pastoring at Freedom Temple – Carbondale, and his desire is to have Darrien step up to the plate as the pastor of the church. The pastor wanted to make the transition as smooth as possible, so he called the board of elders in for counsel. And Mother Smith over here has informed us that, according to the bylaws of the church, the pastor needs to be married, so..." Lady Roberts said.

"So, I wanted to know how you would feel about expediting this wedding so that I can take over the church," Darrien blurted out.

"Wait, what?" Shyanne was flabbergasted. It was already happening; her greatest fear was already happening. Their lives were already revolving around the church, and they had not even said 'I do'.

"Babe, we were getting married anyway; so, I just wanted to know if we could speed up the process," Darrien said. He could hardly look her in the eye. He saw the steam rising from the top of her head and he knew she was pissed.

"Let's talk in the hallway. Now." Shyanne said to him through gritted teeth.

Shyanne and Darrien excused themselves from the room and went into the hall.

"Darrien, what the heck was that? And why would you put me on the spot like that and ask me in front of all those people?"

"Those people are our family."

"No, those people are our family AND those random church folks. I have never met those people a day in my life, but they felt comfortable enough to tell me when I need to get married?" Shyanne said.

"Shyanne, I apologize that I asked you in front of everybody, but you know what I'm trying to do for my Dad. If it were you, I would be with it," Darrien said.

"I did not make a statement to let you know whether or not I was with it. All I'm saying is, if we're going to be a team, we need to communicate. You have dedicated yourself to all of this without uttering a word to me and asking me how I felt. When you said 'yes,' you did not just commit for you, you committed for me, too. If we're going to do life together, let's do it together. That's not fair, man. We have been engaged for three days and you're already letting the church run our lives. I'm not happy about that!" Shyanne snapped.

Darrien wanted to be upset at her for raising her voice, but Shyanne was absolutely right. He had made a decision for her without her input and it was not fair. "You're right, babe. I really feel like I'm called to be a pastor and I also want to help my father. If you could please be on board and have a quickie wedding with me, I promise you for our one-year anniversary, I will give you the biggest wedding of your dreams. Just please, help me out," Darrien begged.

Shyanne looked deeply into his eyes. She wanted to stay upset, but Shyanne had wanted to be married her whole life. She loved Darrien and wanted to be his wife; she just had to put her foot down about her feelings. She finally broke the silence by saying, "fine; but my family and friends need to be out here for this quick ceremony. I want a new white dress for it. We're going to do it in the chapel downstairs. We're going to have the reception in your Dad's suite, and my dad is going to officiate; ok?"

"I got you," Darrien said as he picked her up and held her close.

"And Darrien," she said, tapping him on the shoulder.

"Yes?"

"We need to get a house because I'm not living in your bachelor's pad."

Chapter 25

Selena was at Shyanne's house in disbelief at what she was seeing on the television. She did not know if she should be flattered or angry.

Everybody knows Selena loved her some Oprah. One of her cousins had gifted her Oprah's twentieth anniversary DVDs for Christmas one year, and Selena literally made everyone sit up and watch the entire DVD series on the holiday. When Oprah linked back up with one of her show's former life coaches for her twenty-fifth anniversary and farewell season, Selena was in full-blown heaven.

Now, she sat in Selena's living room with a pint of Cake Batter ice cream, watching last weekend's episode of folks getting their lives fixed. Selena rarely got to watch television these days because she was so busy with Pizazz. In fact, she was going to ask her sister if she could become part owner in the near future. Selena did so much work at Pizazz and she wanted a piece of that pie. As Selena went to the recorded television programs, she read the "info" section of the episode. It informed her that the episode would be about Ms. V putting four Black men into a house of healing dealing with their familial and relationship issues.

Interested, Selena pressed play. What she saw next took her to infinity and beyond.

After the opening song and sequence, the show introduced the audience to four Black men who wanted Ms. V to fix their lives. Their names were Troy, Joshua, Darius, and Kyle. Yes, Selena's Kyle. Selena was floored. She did not care about any of the other three men's experiences, she wanted to get into what Kyle was saying.

"Why am I here beloved?" Ms. V asked him in a sweet, motherly tone.

"Well, I'm here at the House of Healing because I need you to fix my life, Ms. V. I lost the love of my life, and I can't get over it," Kyle said genuinely.

Selena watched on with her mouth wide open.

"What do you mean when you say, 'lost the love of your life?' Is he or she dead? Did he or she leave you? Let's be clear," Ms. V inquired.

"She left me."

"Negro, I didn't just leave you," Selena yelled to the television. "Tell her you were blowing my best friend's back out. Don't put that on me!"

"Ah," Ms. V paused.

Kyle dropped his head and began to cry.

"What is that, beloved? Why are we in tears? Can we get Sir Kyle some tissue, please?"

"She left me because I cheated on her and I hate that I messed up, and I would do anything to get her back," Kyle said.

Tears began to form in Selena's eyes.

"Mmm... So, you betrayed her. Can you own that?" Ms. V said.

"Yes."

"Say that for me. I betrayed the love of my life."

"I..." Kyle stammered.

"I betrayed the love of my life. You're going to have to sit in that. Come on, say it," Ms. V said as she got up to sit directly in his face.

"I betrayed the love of my life," Kyle said.

"And my actions drove her away."

"And my actions drove her away," Kyle said it and broke down. The reality of what he had done had never been spoken from his lips until that very moment, but Ms. V sensed there was more to say.

"See, that's good because saying 'she left me' puts the blame on her. Let's just make it about you. You understand what I mean?" Ms. V said.

Kyle nodded his head yes.

"I want you to take some deep breaths, Kyle. Come on, breathe in and breathe out for me." Ms. V took one hand and placed it on his diaphragm and coached him through breathing techniques. "Ok, Kyle, I am sensing something. And I want you to be honest with yourself and with me. Because women will rarely leave on the first indiscretion. Why did she really leave, beloved? It wasn't the cheating. What was it?"

"I betrayed her by cheating with her friend," Kyle said and broke down to his knees.

For some reason, seeing Kyle in such a break down caused Selena to cry. She had no idea he was that remorseful. She had not heard from him since she Floyd Mayweather'ed Miriam. She always thought it was odd that he never sent her flowers or came by to apologize. Now she could see that he had not begged her forgiveness because he had not yet forgiven himself.

Selena felt something wet on her leg and looked down. It was her ice cream. She hurried, trying to use her fingers to scoop the ice cream back into its container. Shyanne was sure to kill her for getting ice cream on her fur rug.

"Dang it, man!" Selena paused the television to clean up the ice cream as best as she could. After she was done cleaning, there was still a stain on the rug that she could not remove. Selena tried several times to clean the stain, but she could not. She eventually gave up and put the cleaning supplies away; she'd just have to deal with her sister later. She sat back in her original seat and resumed the episode.

"Wow, beloved. We're going to unpack that; ok," Ms. V said.

She then began to deal with another one of her guests. Selena could care less about the nice-looking gentleman. She fast forwarded to Kyle's part.

"Kyle, tell me about your father. What did he teach you about being a man?" Ms. V asked.

"Well, he taught me that it was a man's job to provide for his family. My father did not live with us, but whatever we needed, he got it for us."

"So, your father was not emotionally available, but he was financially providing for you all?"

"I guess so," Kyle said.

"No. It's a yes or no, beloved. Was he emotionally there for you or not?"

"No, ma'am," Kyle said.

"Ok, now breathe. You're doing good," Ms. V coached him.

"So, why did your parents not live together? Were they divorced?"

"No, they did not live together because my father and his wife and family lived across the street. He lived with his family," Kyle said matter-of-factly, as if it were normal.

"His family? Were you not his family, beloved?" Ms. V asked.

"No. I was his child, but I was not a part of his family," Kyle said with tears in his eyes.

"Whoa! That was big! Did you all hear that? So, your Daddy taught you that a man could love you and hold you across the street. He can be with you, produce with you, and still not be there for you. No wonder why you cheated, baby. The pathology continues. You did what you saw," Ms. V said.

Selena had known Kyle for years, but she had no idea he had experienced such trauma in his childhood. She knew about his mother being the other woman, but she did not realize that he was living in a cycle his parents created for him.

Selena cried as Kyle broke down on the television.

"Come here, baby. Just sit right here on my lap. You're not a thirty-year-old man, you're still the seven-year-old boy seeing his father go home to his family across the street, beloved. You just need to be held by your mama."

Kyle continued to sit on her lap.

"Just let your heart break for the little boy," Ms. V said as she rubbed his back. "Kyle, of course you were not faithful, baby. You did not know how to be faithful. You did what you were taught. But now that you know better, you can break the generational curse."

Selena turned the television off. What she loved is, Ms. V did not blame her or Kyle's parents for his actions. He now had the choice, and Ms. V would give him the tools, to end the pathology.

Selena got up and paced back and forth on the living room floor. She felt like this was the best time where she could get closure. Just as she was thinking, her phone started vibrating. Selena looked down at her phone and noticed it was Shyanne calling.

"Hello," Selena answered dryly.

"I'm getting married!" Shyanne squealed in excitement.

"Wasn't I there when Darrien proposed?" Selena retorted.

"Yes; but what I mean is, we're getting married Friday at noon."

"WHAT? Why would you get married Friday, Shyanne? So, y'all won't even be engaged for a week? That's crazy!" Selena said.

"We're getting married here at the hospital because Darrien's father is retiring from the pastorate, and in order for Darrien to pastor the church, he has to be married."

"Shyanne, you're making my head hurt. You're going from talking, to dating for two seconds, to married in two minutes. You don't even want to be a first lady. And what about Pizazz?"

Shyanne took a deep breath. She knew she was pushing it with her next request, but she needed her sister. "I was going to ask you if you would take on my duties while I'm gone. I will have to hire someone else to help you out, but I do want you to run it. No one can nail my vision like my sister. I'm not neglecting my boutique, but I won't be there daily. Can you please help?"

"Shyanne, the only way I'm running this store for you is if we have an agreement. I need to be forty percent owner of Pizazz. I put in work; I order supplies; I have gone from supporting your dream to taking on your dream as if it were my own. I'm only doing it if I get to be part owner. If not, find someone else or close the doors," Selena said and hung up.

She was already emotional from watching the episode of Fix My Life, then her sister just had to call her needing a favor. Selena was tired of being there for Shyanne and coming up empty.

She loved her sister, but she needed a break. Selena blocked her sister's phone number. She would surely unblock her tomorrow, but she needed peace today.

Her mind traveled back to Kyle. She scrolled through her contact list and landed on his name, "Kyle". Selena pondered whether she wanted to speak to him. She decided to go ahead and call him. She pressed the green button to dial him up, then ended the call after swiftly deciding she was a fool.

"Think, Selena! Do not call him," she encouraged herself.

Two seconds later, Kyle was dialing her back. She took a deep breath and answered the phone. She did not say a word.

"Hello?" Kyle said. He was both grateful and staggered to receive her phone call. He figured she had seen Fix My Life and wanted to talk about it.

The sound of Kyle's voice alone caused a single tear to roll down Selena's cheek. She had not heard that sound in months. She craved the sound of his voice, but his choices had stifled its sweet sound and rendered him silent.

"I need to talk Friday at two o'clock at the Starbucks by Shy's house," Selena said and hung up. She ran to the bathroom, leaned over the toilet, and began to regurgitate. Her nerves had gotten the best of her; but in two days, she was going to get all the clarity and closure her heart desired.

Chapter 26

The next day, on the eve of the wedding, everyone was in Carbondale, with the exception of Selena, who said she would stay back at Pizazz and catch the hospital ceremony on Facetime. Shyanne knew better. She knew her sister was upset with her and overwhelmed, but she was grateful that Selena had decided to keep the doors of her boutique open. Shyanne had decided to allow her sister to become co-owner of the boutique. It was only fair. Instead of the forty percent Selena asked for, Shyanne had her lawyers draw up paperwork that would give Selena fifty percent of the boutique. Selena was elated but she still needed a break.

Back at the hospital, everyone took around-the-clock care of Bishop Roberts, who could not be more excited about his son's impending nuptials.

Shyanne was putting the final touches on her hospital wedding. She and her mother had picked up her dress, shoes, a cake, and arranged for the Baja Fresh, one of the restaurants in the hospital's cafeteria, to prepare a taco bar for the celebration.

"Lisa, when are you going to let me take you out?" Rashawn asked.

"I'm not. You cannot handle a woman like me, Rashawn. I'm not as saved as you. I'm not waiting until marriage. I date multiple men at once, and I do me," Lisa said with confidence.

"Well, I think I can handle a woman like you. I think you're scared of a man like me," he countered.

"Scared of what? And for what? Because you're a church boy?" Lisa waved him off. "Been there, done that."

"Exactly. Who hurt you? And why are you afraid to be a good girl? Because you're not as tough as you put on. You wear bad girl like it's a badge of honor, but I can look in your eyes and see that all of what you're doing is not making you happy. So, why don't you take a chance with this church boy? I won't bite," Rashawn said.

"But, I might."

"Whatever, man. You're my date to the wedding tomorrow so be ready to dance and exchange numbers," Rashawn said as he walked away.

Shyanne saw their conversation and chuckled to herself. Anyone with two eyes could see the heat radiating off of them. She could not wait until Lisa let her wall down and stopped using dating and sex as a defense mechanism. She'd learn one day though.

Just as Shyanne was thinking about Lisa and Rashawn, her youngest sister, Skylar, came up and sat next to her. Skylar looked up to Shyanne more than she'd ever know.

"Hey, Shy."

"Hey, my Sky," Shyanne said with a smile. She loved her entire family and felt so blessed to have them all the time.

"Are you excited for the mini-wedding tomorrow?"

"I'm big excited. But I'm more excited about the wedding next year. I can't wait to have the big ole wedding with the huge gown and everything."

"Me too. Well, I just wanted you to know that I love you and I think Darrien is a good dude; so, I look forward to him being my brother. Do not mess up with this guy," Skylar said.

"No, you mean to tell him not to mess up with me," Shyanne said with her hand on her chest as she clutched her invisible pearls.

"No. I meant what I said. I already threatened Darrien. It was your turn," Skylar said in all seriousness.

"Girl get up out of my face!"

Skylar laughed and walked off. She loved to rile Shyanne up. It was like her second job.

"Skylar, stop acting crazy," she heard her father say behind her. He had decided to come and take this moment to speak to his daughter. She was the first one of his kids to get married. Although the setting was not the best, the love was pure. Bishop Lawson had observed Darrien since he was a child. He was raised to be a good man. And as the Bible instructed, he loved Shy like Christ loved the church, inside and outside of her presence.

"Baby."

"Yes, sir?" Shyanne said.

"You're going to be somebody's wife tomorrow. And a stunning wife at that," Bishop Lawson said.

"Thank you, Daddy."

"God is going to bless you. You've always been obedient; you're smart, loving, and you put God first. No matter what, know that God is with you and He will bless you and Darrien's union."

"I believe that. Thanks, Old Man," Shyanne said as she got up and hugged her dad.

"You know I love you, right?"

"Yes, sir, without a doubt." Shyanne and her father hugged each other. Bishop was almost more excited than Shyanne was. One would think it was him walking down the aisle. But who could blame him for his excitement? He had groomed his daughter to be a boss, and she was just that. She had her own boutique, her own house, her own style, her own personality—she was her own woman. Although he did not think Darrien would leave Shyanne, the fact is that they were not co-dependent, they were interdependent. If Darrien lost his mind today or tomorrow and left her, Shyanne would be hurt; but she would be ok. That's the kind of woman he raised.

"Excuse me, I don't mean to interrupt but I would like to speak to the bride in private," Lady Eva said.

"Sure thing, honey," Bishop said and offered his wife a tender kiss on the forehead.

Shyanne braced herself for a conversation with her mother. They rarely spoke one-on-one. Shyanne took a sharp, deep breath and said, "What's up, ma?"

"Let's go over there and have a seat."

They went over to an area of the waiting room that was concentrated with fewer people. She wanted to speak to her daughter without a lot of people listening.

"Shyanne, I wanted to tell you that I love you. I have always loved you and I always will," Lady Eva said softly.

"I love you, too, Mama. I have never doubted your love for me. I know you love me, even if you're as tough as nails."

Lady Eva shook her head. Although Shyanne was her child, she really had no idea who her mother really was on the inside. She was not hard or tough, she was as soft as cotton. Often times, her tough words were the wall she had built so no one could harm her. She had not realized, until it was too late, that she had kept the façade of the tough exterior in front of Shyanne, prohibiting her from penetrating her heart.

"I'm really not that tough, Shyanne. I know I seem like it, but I'm not. I cry a lot. Especially when we get into it. It actually does affect me, and I know it has an effect on you, too. I know it may seem too late in the game, but I really pray and hope we can actually get to know each other," Lady Eva said sincerely.

"It's not too late, Ma," Shyanne said as she hugged her mother.

291

"I've loved you since I brought you home from the hospital. You were born three months early. You had all kinds of tubes attached to you, but you were my chocolate baby. I was just exhausted having you and Lena. I cried all the time. Your cry was so high pitched, it pierced my eardrums. I just felt like it was all my fault that you weren't born perfect. I hated myself for not being able to bring you to term. Your dad was so protective of you, but I loved you, too. But I struggled with that postpartum depression for real. I had to know that you were born incomplete—no matter what was wrong. Shyanne, you are perfect in whatever stage you're in. I love you and I know you will be the perfect wife."

Shyanne began to cry. She had fists full of tears. She had never heard her mother speak so lovingly about her. It was a beautiful surprise. Shyanne made the decision that she would try her hardest to create a better relationship with her mother. Lady Eva had poured her heart out to Shyanne and she was not going to stomp on it in return—she would grant her mother's request. The two ladies parted ways as Darrien came over to speak to his bride.

"Everything ok?" Darrien asked.

"Yes, everything is great. I'm excited to become one with you in about twenty-six more hours," Shyanne said.

"Same here. Now, here are the keys to my parents' house. You, your mom, Skylar, and Lisa are going to sleep there tonight," Darrien said and handed her the keys. Kyra and Cole had already gotten a hotel room nearby.

"Why?"

"Because I'm not supposed to see you twenty-four hours before the wedding," Darrien reminded her.

"Oh, right. Ok; see you tomorrow. I know you're going to be fine as chilled wine tomorrow."

"Naw, I'm looking forward to seeing this dress. Whatever you wear, I know it's going to be beautiful," Darrien said. "Goodnight, beautiful."

"Goodnight, Future." They embraced one last time as fiancés. Shyanne turned to Lisa and said, "Round up the troops, it's time to go."

When they arrived at the Roberts' house, Shyanne instantly felt welcomed and loved. The entire home was decorated in earth tones. With all the paintings and a few statement chandeliers, Shyanne felt like she was at a hotel. The house had three bedrooms, three baths, a full basement that had another half bathroom, living room, dining room, kitchen, theater room, laundry room, and den. Shyanne could see herself at the Roberts' home for holidays and birthdays for sure. The house was not huge; but it was a nice, family home.

She decided that she, her mom, and Lisa and Skylar would all sleep in the basement together. They got covers from the laundry room and turned the basement into a big slumber party. They talked all night, ordered pizza, and watched all of Shyanne's favorite movies. They even Facetime'd Selena.

"Hey, Lena Wena," Lisa said as Selena answered the phone.

"Hey! Hey, everybody!" Selena waved into the phone.

"Hey!" Everyone said in unison.

"Shyanne are you excited?" Selena asked.

"Girl, yeah. I probably won't be able to sleep tonight. This is better than Christmas."

"Good. Well, congratulations to you, sis. Oh, and before I forget, has anybody watched television out there lately?" Selena asked.

"No," everyone said.

"Girl, I've just been at the hospital for a few days. Bishop Roberts does not really like to watch a bunch of tv; so, no. What did we miss?" Shyanne asked and waited with baited breath for the response.

"Baby, you missed Fix My Life!"

Everyone was completely let down by Selena's revelation. They could care less about watching the show.

"Girl, I know that that's your show and all, but we do not care. We were sitting up here thinking you were talking about something juicy and you're talking about Ms. V? Go to bed!" Lisa quarreled.

"Excuse you, it was juicy. Kyle was on there. Bam, I said it!"

"Kyle who?" Skylar shrieked.

"My former Kyle."

"Lord, Jesus," Lady Eva whispered.

Selena told them all about the episode but conveniently skipped out on telling the part about deciding to meet up with him for 'closure'. She knew she needed the closure, but she also knew that her family and friends would never understand anyway. But tomorrow was the day. She had to do it.

Chapter 27

"**B**aby, can you believe they are going to go through with this wedding?" Kyra asked her husband, Cole. The pair were in their hotel suite's bathroom. Kyra was offered to lodge at Darrien's parents' place, but she politely declined. She was not about to spend the night apart from her husband, and especially not in an unfamiliar location where someone else had the keys. No thank you.

"Not this soon I can't, but it does not matter. We do not have to agree with their timeline; we just need to support them by being here; and if they ask us for advice, we can give it to them."

"You're right, babe. That's why I love you—you're so wise," she said as she paused the application of her makeup and made out with her husband. Cole grabbed her by her waist and kissed her back with twice the intensity. The two finally came up for air after minutes of nonstop making out. Cole eyed his wife's swollen lips.

"If you were not already pregnant, I would put a baby in you tonight," Cole joked. "You look really good."

"Thanks, love. I was going to tell everybody about the baby this week, but I'll wait for a couple more months. I do not want to overstep my boundaries and take over Shyanne's day," Kyra said.

"Good idea."

Kyra was three months pregnant with her first child. She had not begun to show yet. The only people who know about the pregnancy were she and her husband. Kyra found out she was pregnant over breakfast. Although Kyra was late getting her menstrual cycle, she did not think it was anything more than the fact that she was stressed out.

One day, Cole brought her some breakfast from VO's, a soul food restaurant on the west side of Chicago. They both loved VO's. Kyra loved breakfast food, period. When he brought it into the house, Kyra messed that food up. She practically inhaled the large pancakes, ham and cheese omelet, bacon, sausage, and hash browns. The sausage and hash browns weren't even for her, they were for Cole. Kyra was not paying any attention. She was just gobbling up the food.

When Cole mentioned how much and how quickly she had eaten, she was immediately offended to the point of tears. Cole had never made any comments on her weight or the way she had eaten before. She was heartbroken, but she had to admit he was right, and that was not like Kyra.

The next morning, she woke up incredibly dizzy and nauseated. Between nausea, large intakes of food, and mood swings, Kyra feared she had the flu. However, when she went to the doctor to be checked out, she was informed that she was in fact pregnant.

Kyra was overjoyed. She and Cole had not been trying to have a baby, but they weren't not trying either. She decided to get a cake from the bakery Cake Girls, and when Cole came home from work, she told him that she had purchased a cake that was in the kitchen. He went into the kitchen, and when he saw the cake on the table, he was beyond thrilled. The cake was shaped like an oven, and it had a small bun inside, which signified they had a bun in the oven. They were excited to share the news with the world; but for now, it was Shyanne's day.

"Cole, I'm so glad you've been so supportive during this whole pregnancy thing. I really have the best husband in the world."

"And I have the best wife."

"And I cannot believe my Best is about to become a wife. I mean, don't get me wrong, I want her to be married; but not like this. You're getting married just because your man needs a First Lady? I just don't know about all of this, and I'm concerned in real life," Kyra said.

"Kyra, we're minding our business. Now, come on and get ready, so we can get to this hospital."

In the neurology unit's first floor ladies' room, which also doubled as Shyanne's bridal suite, she put on the finishing touches to her makeup. "You cute, girl," she said to herself as she looked into the mirror.

Lisa came into the bathroom in awe of her friend's beauty. Shyanne was not even dressed yet, but her beauty was simply radiant.

"Friend, you are stunning," Lisa said as she began to tear up.

"I know Easy L ain't crying! Not you! You're the Rock of Gibraltar," Shyanne joked.

"Girl, shut up. I am human sometimes, you know."

"Yes, I know. I want you to know it though."

"Listen, today is not psychoanalyze Lisa day; this is your day. And you are going to rock it. So, go ahead and finish your makeup so we can get you in this dress. You're already running late."

"Yeah, yeah, yeah. Come back in twenty minutes so you can help me get dressed," Shyanne instructed.

"I got you." Lisa turned to leave.

Shyanne looked down at her phone and noticed a text from Darrien. He simply told her he could not wait to marry her. Shyanne would cherish their love forever. She sent him a heart and continued to beat her face.

Five minutes later, Lady Eva came into the bathroom to ask if she were almost ready. Shyanne purposely did not get agitated by everyone and their sudden need to rush her. They had already rushed this date, and they were not going to rush her.

"I'll be done in a minute, mom."

"Ok; just making sure. We're all just so excited. And so is Darrien. He looks so dapper."

"I'm sure he does. I can't wait to see him. If you could, would you go get Kyra and Lisa and ask them to come here."

"Sure."

Moments later, Kyra and Lisa came into the restroom.

"Can you ladies help me with getting dressed?"

"Sure," Lisa said. She was so bright-eyed and excited for her friend.

"Yeah," Kyra replied.

Shyanne wore a Ramona Keveza bridal jumpsuit. When she was asked what color dress she would be wearing, she immediately exclaimed "White!" Shyanne had earned her white dress. She opted for a jumpsuit since the setting was less formal. The jumpsuit had a deep, plunging neckline that came down to showcase a little cleavage but not too much. The top was a halter that showed off her toned back, and the bodice showcased her snatched waist. The jumpsuit fit like a glove, showcasing her amply curvy, but fit, body. Around her waist was a gold belt that her tulle train extended from. On her feet, she wore clear Louboutin's, styled with jewels and crystals. Her natural hair was in Darrien's favorite style on her, an afro.

Kyra and Lisa were stunned. They had never seen their friend show so much skin in their lives. She looked beautiful.

Kyra began to put the flowers into her best friend's hair. "Best friend."

"Yes, Best?"

"Are you sure you're ready to do this? Because either way, I'm here for you. We can get in the car and go home right now, or we can do this thing. What's up?"

Shyanne looked into the mirror and spotted Kyra's eyes. "The only thing I have been surer of is that Jesus is Lord."

"Boom, that's all I needed to know. Let's get you married," Kyra said.

Lisa was so happy Kyra had dropped the issue. Everyone already knew how Kyra felt. Everyone knew she thought Shyanne and Darrien should wait, but it was not her decision. Kyra just had to be quiet and let the couple make their own decisions. Heck, when Kyra got married in Bishop Lawson's office, it was not the ideal wedding, but everyone supported Kyra. It was time for her to do the same.

"Ok, Lisa, can you go tell my Daddy 'nem to get in place so we can start this wedding?"

Freedom Temple – Carbondale's board members were in the chapel waiting for the wedding to begin. Bishop Darrien Roberts, Sr., was wheeled down in his wheelchair to the chapel. He sat adjacent to the front row on the right-hand side. Next, his Lady Roberts walked down the aisle and sat next to her husband. After the Roberts were seated, Lady Eva came down the aisle and was seated in the front row on the left-hand of the chapel.

Next, Darrien came walking down the aisle looking like a whole GQ model. He wore a black and white paisley print, velvet jacket, white shirt, black slacks, and black suede shoes. He looked quite spiffy.

It was clear that Darrien had been crying. His eyes were red and puffy. He was emotional because he could not believe the day had come that he would be marrying the love of his life.

With the sounds of Syleena Johnson's song, "Classic Love Song" playing on Tim's phone, the wedding party filed in. The party consisted of Skylar walking arm in arm with Steven, Jr., Rashawn and Lisa, and Kyra and Cole. The entire wedding party wore black and white. The ladies had on red shoes. It was not too bad for two-day planning.

Marvin came up in front of the chapel and addressed the audience. "The Bible says, 'Whoso findeth a wife findeth a good thing, and obtaineth favor of the Lord' in Proverbs 18:22. I am grateful that my friend and favor has truly found God's favor in Shyanne. I thank her for being my sister. And now what God has joined together, no man shall put asunder. Please, stand as we receive our bride. Hit it, Tim."

Tim began to play Donny Hathaway's hit "Love, Love, Love." When Donny started singing the words, "Aww baby, you make me fall in love with you," the chapel's doors swung open and Bishop Lawson and Shyanne began walking down the aisle. Bishop Lawson was in tears, but no one was more awestruck than Darrien.

Shyanne's radiant beauty knocked the wind out of Darrien. He stood at the altar doing the manliest cry he could muster up as Shyanne glided to him. It was reminiscent of the cry Will Smith's character did when he found out he had the job in the Pursuit of Happiness movie.

When Bishop Lawson and Shyanne got to the altar, Shyanne and Darrien took each other's hands. Bishop Lawson stepped in front of them and said, "Ladies and gentlemen, we are gathered here today to join this man and this woman in holy matrimony. We know no one would be brave enough to object; so, we can move on."

Everyone laughed at the Bishop's humor.

"This couple has written their own vows, or at least, they're going to make them up right now. Darrien."

"Shyanne, or my Shy, as I like to call you. I love you from my core. You are my best friend. I vow to keep you second, only to God. I vow to value your word and opinion. I vow to not move without you. I vow to be your partner. I vow to love you as Christ loved the church. And I vow to give you as many babies as you want."

"Don't nobody need to hear that, boy," Bishop Roberts said, and the audience doubled over in laughter.

"I vow to be a man worth submitting to. I vow to love, honor, cherish and obey. I vow to keep falling in love with you every day."

The audience was filled with tears and oohs and ahs.

"Shyanne," Bishop Lawson said.

"Darrien, I love you and I thank you for loving me. You, too, are my best friend. I vow to keep you second, only to God. I vow to be agreeable and teachable. I vow to not make you responsible for my happiness. I vow to not blame you for my insecurities, but I will be happy and share my happiness with you. I will not put that pressure on you and treat you as if you are God. It is not your job to fix me; it is your job to grow with me in Him. I vow to be yours and only yours. I vow to submit to the mission God has given you for our family. I vow to love, honor, cherish and obey. I vow to keep falling in love with you every day."

There was not a dry eye in the chapel. Everyone there knew either Shyanne or Darrien since they were children. To see them as adults, basking in love, was a remarkable sight.

"Such beautiful vows. Marriage and love is a choice. You must choose each other over other people, over the church, over opinions, choose each other. Your love, in its purest form, is a reflection of God's love for you and your love for God. If you neglect your spouse, you are neglecting God. I do not care how many hours you spend in church, if you dishonor your spouse, you are dishonoring God. Keep your relationship with your spouse at the forefront of your mind as an act of worship to God for taking out the time to handmake a gift like your spouse just for you. Say amen, somebody," Bishop Lawson said.

The entire audience said "Amen," in agreement. Even Selena said "amen," from the Facetime call on her mother's phone.

"Now, let me see the rings." Rashawn pulled both platinum wedding bands out of his suit jacket pocket and handed them to the Bishop.

"The rings are a circle; they symbolize the love you have for each other and for God, a love that never ends. And right now, we're going to ask Bishop Roberts if he will pray over these rings and this union," Bishop Lawson said.

"Let's all bow our heads. Lord, we thank You for this day that you had in mind from the beginning of time. You knew what would be before it was. You know what will be before it is. We pray in your name that you will bless this union. Remind them to keep you at the center. We bind every distraction, every naysayer, every trap that the enemy set—it will not work. This union will last. Their love will last. Their joy will last. And we thank You for it even now. In Jesus' name, amen!"

"Amen!"

"And now, by the power vested in me by God and the state of Illinois, I now pronounce you man and wife; you may kiss your bride."

Darrien eyed Shyanne hungrily and dove in. The small audience cheered and cheered for their union. It was the happiest day of their lives. Nothing could take away the smile from Shyanne's face.

Chapter 28

It was 2:30 in the afternoon when Selena's Uber pulled up to the Starbucks. Her sister's wedding ceremony had been over for one hour, but for some reason, she could not will herself to open the app and schedule the car service. She wanted to talk to Kyle, but she was honestly nervous. What would she do when she saw him? Would she spaz out and try to stab him? Would she get the answers she wanted? Would he be disrespectful? Regardless, it was now or never.

Selena put on her sunglasses and strutted inside the coffee shop. As soon as she stepped over the threshold, she spotted Kyle. It was crazy how she felt at that moment. Seeing his face made her remember how much she actually loved him, though she wanted to hate him. She swiftly had to check her emotions. Her issue was never love, it was honor and respect. She did not have time to feel in this moment—she was there to get answers.

As Selena approached the table, Kyle stood. He did not know whether he should hug her or not, but Lord knows he wanted to. He decided to greet her with a smile and extended his hand for a handshake. "Good afternoon, Ms. Lawson," he said.

Selena reluctantly shook his hand and said, "hello."

Kyle came around and pulled out her chair for her. Selena was more beautiful than he remembered. She had an effortless, timeless beauty. He knew he had probably ruined their relationship for life; but he felt like she deserved to get her questions answered truthfully, even if the truth hurt his chances in the long run.

"Listen, Kyle. I watched you on Fix My Life, and I don't know how to feel. I mean, I was grateful to see you take responsibility for your actions and not blame me; but I need answers."

"I'm here to answer," Kyle said.

"How long were you and the backstabber messing around?"

"Right at two months. We were not in a relationship. We had sex four times during that time and I regret every moment," Kyle said truthfully.

"I don't need to know what you regret. Please, just answer the questions. I don't need the emotions. When did it start?"

"It started at one of my gigs. I was playing a club and she came in there drunk and sloppy and I started drinking with her. I took her home. I was just trying to make sure she got there safely, and she started kissing me. I dodged it at first; but then, I got into it. I tried to end it that day, but she started blackmailing me and saying she was going to tell you if I did not have sex with her. That's the only reason why it went beyond that first day. I should have manned up and..."

"No," Selena interrupted, "I do not care about what you should have done because you did not do it. When I came to the gym to confront you, your little whore had on lingerie! She was meeting you up there, Kyle! Why did you have her meeting you where you know I would potentially pop up?"

"I did not tell that girl to come up there!"

"Yeah, right," Selena said and rolled her eyes.

"Lena, we are having an open conversation right now. I have not lied to you since we've been here. I have never told this girl where I work out. She was straight stalking me. The only time we had sex was at her place. I was not parading this girl around— everybody knew you were my girl."

"Wait, did you say you never told her where you worked out?" Selena's wheels started turning.

"Yes! I know I messed up, but I was not that bold with it," Kyle said. He looked at her, his eyes pleading for Selena to believe him.

"Oh my God!"

"What?" Kyle said.

"She got your whereabouts from me. I told her I was about to stop by and see you at the gym just about a week before I beat her up. Wow. This chick is twisted," she said.

"Wow."

"Wait a minute. That was the same night I saw somebody in the window at the gym and then they ran off. Miriam was really stalking you?" Selena asked, as she began to put two and two together.

"Yes! Those pictures you saw on my phone was her sending me pictures. I never sent her any nor did I reply!" Kyle said.

Selena started to think. He was telling the truth. Tears began to flow from her eyes. It was amazing how you can be best friends with a person's representative, not knowing that they were a whole 'nother person privately.

"I'm sorry for crying. I just can't believe I was friends with this girl. Like, I don't even know her, and I thought I did," Selena cried.

"Man, I'm sorry." Kyle got up and wrapped his arms around Selena. He knew what Miriam had done did not erase his actions—he was not innocent—but all the blame was not his either.

"Ok, I'm good," Selena said as she sat up and wiped her face. "Is there anything else I need to know?"

Kyle pondered whether or not he should tell her about the baby. He did not want to keep any secrets from her, but he also did not want to hurt her.

"Yeah, there is one more thing," Kyle took a deep breath. "I always used protection with that girl; but do you remember when you were fighting, and she was bleeding?"

"Yeah, so?"

"So, after the fight, she told me that when you were fighting her..."

"You're lying," Selena interrupted him.

310

"She said that she miscarried during the fight and the baby was mine. I do not know if the baby was actually mine because I'm telling you, I stayed strapped up, but she did have a miscarriage. That is a fact."

Selena was crushed. Her former best friend and her man possibly created a life together? What in the Love and Hip-Hop foolishness was going on with her life?

"Did you love her?" Selena asked.

"I have only been in love with one woman in my entire life, and her name is Selena Gizelle Lawson. And Miriam knows that. She was angry with me because I told her that my heart only belonged to you and I was not interested in being anything on any level with her. I don't even know if I believe the whole baby thing. I just want her to stay away from me. She is a psycho, for real," Kyle said, honestly.

"Ok. Kyle, I believe you. I do not want to be in a relationship with you, but I do want us to be cordial. I cannot keep harboring hateful feelings towards you. I just can't do it. It's making me sick," Selena said.

"Lena, all I wanted to do was reconcile. I wanted you to hear my side. I hurt you—I know I did—but I did not seek out to hurt you. Selena, I apologize deeply and whatever you need me to do to make it better, I will."

"Well, you can give me a hug and we will work on the rest later," Selena said.

The two of them embraced. Selena was happy to have gotten closure. She did not know if she would ever want to speak to Kyle again; but for right now, she got what she needed.

"Can I take a picture with you? I want to send it to the girls," Selena said, referring to Shyanne, Kyra, and Lisa.

"Sure."

The pair smiled for the photo. Both of their eyes were puffy and sore from crying. You could not deny that they still loved each other; but sometimes, when you love something, you just have to let it go.

"Hey, Lena," Kyle called out as she was about to leave Starbucks.

"Yeah?"

"Send me that picture on Snapchat. And thank you for the reconciliation."

Selena smiled and turned to leave.

Chapter 29

I
t was a brisk Saturday afternoon. The sun was shining, and birds were chirping. It was partly cloudy, but it felt good outside. Meanwhile, there was a dark cloud over the Austin community. Miriam lie at home on her mother's couch. She was channel surfing on the television. She settled on watching TV One's Fatal Attraction. It had become one of Miriam's favorite shows.

"Oh, they look so happy," Ms. Black said to herself as she walked into the living room.

"Who?" Miriam inquired.

"Oh, Shyanne and Darrien tied the knot and I'm looking at the pictures on Instagram."

"Oh," Miriam focused her attention back to the television. On the screen was a story about a man who had barbequed his ex. These types of stories used to give Miriam nightmares and stomach aches; but now, she was desensitized.

Miriam's mother desperately wanted her to get back to her normal self. But Miriam would never return. She watched the television with a distant look in her eyes. She was there, but she really was not.

Miriam looked over at her mother's face, which still had a smirk on it. Miriam decided to look at the photos herself. She grabbed her phone and logged into Instagram. All her former friends and Kyle had her blocked on all forms of social media; but she could find them on her alternative account, @KylMiKhy. The name was a summation of the names Kyle, Miriam, and their deceased child, Khy.

Miriam logged on and went right to Shyanne's page. Her bridal jumpsuit thing was cute, but she was surprised she had not had a big wedding. Shyanne had talked about getting married their entire lives. She scrolled and scrolled through the photos, but she did not see any photos of Selena. She knew Selena would not miss her sister's wedding. She searched for Selena's page, and her heart skipped two beats. Miriam held her chest because she just knew she was about to have a heart attack. The last photo Selena had posted was a picture of her and Kyle and the caption read "This is what real reconciliation looks like #WalkingInLove." Miriam grew dizzy and nauseous.

She ran to the bathroom to go vomit. Miriam hurled all the food she had eaten. Her eyes were red with anger. If Kyle was going to reconcile with anyone, it should have been her, the mother of his deceased child. Why did he need to make up with the woman who killed their baby?

Miriam stood upright and began to pace back and forth. She had not even thought to brush her teeth, she was that angry.

She pulled out the phone again and studied the picture. It was taken at Starbucks one day prior.

That's it, she thought to herself. Miriam was tired of the disrespect. Selena had to get dealt with, and she had to get dealt with soon.

Selena and Kirsten were completing their customers for the day. It had been a good Saturday at work. Since Selena's conversation with Kyle, she felt like a load had been lifted off her shoulders. She had cried her last tear over Miriam. The truth was, she never knew the girl; she only knew who Miriam allowed her to see.

Selena made a vow to herself that she would not allow Miriam's crazy to penetrate her life. She was done carrying that baggage. Selena was glad that closing time was coming up soon. Lisa and Kyra were supposed to come over to Pizazz to dish about the wedding.

About ten minutes after closing, Kyra and Lisa came knocking on the door. Selena let them in and they all went to her office, including Kirsten. Selena popped a bottle of wine and they all drank it and spilled the tea.

"Girl, it was beautiful," Lisa gushed, "the wedding ceremony was about fifteen minutes. You know Bishop Roberts is still in the hospital; so, we couldn't be all day; but it was good."

"It was and Shy looked great. I can't wait to see what she's going to look like next year at the real wedding," Kyra said.

"Yes, I can't wait!" Selena said, "speaking of, let me call Shyanne."

"Baby, I would be surprised if she answered the phone. She getting to Biblically know her man," Kyra teased.

"Yes, that's why I'm calling," Selena said.

When Shyanne's voicemail picked up, Selena left a short but hilarious voicemail. "Hey, Shy. It's Lena. I was just calling to see if it hurt. Ok, bye!"

"Girl, you are stupid!" Lisa said and fell out laughing.

Kyra, Kirsten, and Selena were cracking up.

"Well, I'm glad you guys made it back to the city safely. We've got to get out of here. We all have church in the morning," Selena said, as she ushered everyone out of her office. She went back to Shyanne's house in a great mood, and she could not wait to see her parents at church in the morning.

Miriam did not sleep the entire night; she was up plotting and planning. She knew Selena like she knew the back of her hand. They were best friends at one point, after all. At seven o'clock in the morning, Miriam went into her mother's room to inform her that she was going to church today. Ms. Black was so excited that Miriam was leaving the house. She had not been outdoors since she was released from the hospital.

Miriam grabbed her car keys and headed for her car. She put the key in the ignition and headed to Shyanne's house. Miriam parked one block away from Shyanne's home and just waited. She had on all black; she had a ski mask, brass knuckles, a bat and a knife. She did not know what the result of this good Sunday would be, but she was prepared for whatever.

Selena walked back and forth in the house. She had a bad feeling. She did not know what was wrong, but she felt like she should stay home today. She then thought about how her father would ring her neck if she was not at church, and quickly decided to go. She called her sister on the phone for some encouragement. This was Shyanne's first Sunday as First Lady and she was excited and nervous about it.

"Hello," Shyanne answered.

"Hey, how are you?"

"I'm good. Listen, I did want to say hi, but I have to get in the sanctuary; so, I'll hit you later." And just like that, Shyanne hung up.

It really hurt Selena's feeling that she would hang up without even saying much. She was getting more and more tired of Shyanne. She decided to call Kyra to get some wisdom on her way out of the door.

"Hello," Kyra answered.

"Hey, First Lady."

Kyra giggled, "Girl, you know you don't have to call me that. How are you?"

"I'm not doing that good. My sister just hung up on me, but I wanted to tell her that I have a really bad feeling about today," Selena locked Shyanne's door and walked to her Uber.

"Hung up on you? Girl, I can't. And bad feeling like what?" Kyra asked.

"Like, I don't know," Selena said as she put her bag in the car. "Like, I feel like something is up—I just don't know what it is."

"Hello, ma'am," the driver said. "Are you Selena?"

"Yes, I am."

And just as Selena's driver was getting ready to take off, the Uber was rear-ended by a champagne-colored car. Selena's head jerked as she hollered aloud.

"Lena! Lena! Lena are you ok?" Kyra asked! "Cole, call 9-1-1! I think Selena's been in an accident in front of Shyanne's house."

As soon as Miriam saw Selena exit Shyanne's house, all she saw was red. *The audacity of this hoe to be walking the streets while my baby is dead!* Miriam thought to herself. Miriam put the pedal to the metal and rear-ended Selena's Uber. When the car jerked, the Uber driver got out of his car hollering and cursing; but Miriam could not hear a word he was saying—she just wanted Selena.

Miriam turned the car off, pulled her ski mask down, hopped out and commenced to go to Selena's side of the car.

Selena was stretching her neck and did not even see the attack coming.

Miriam opened the door, and Selena screamed: "Stop!" Miriam did not stop. She yanked Selena out of the car and began hitting her over and over again in the face with her brass knuckles. Selena just kept screaming, but her screams fueled Miriam's need to feel power. With each blow to Selena's face and back, Miriam chuckled.

The Uber driver ran off after seeing the damage Miriam was doing to his client.

Selena tried to fight back a few times, but she was not able to gain control. As Selena's vision grew blurry, Miriam kicked her in the back of her head. She began to lose consciousness and Miriam took note. She leaned down and whispered in Selena's ear, "Why'd you make me do this to you? Why did you kill my baby?"

Just as Miriam was about to get another lick in, she heard sirens. She ran to her car and left the scene.

Sheridan S. Davis

Chapter 30

I *cannot believe I'm here right now. I hate hospitals.*
I hate these long, everlasting hallways. All I see is
busyness, and a bunch of nameless people walking
up and down these extensive hallways, which seemed to grow
with every step I take. I am so tired of being in hospitals, Shyanne
thought to herself.

"7260. 7260." Shyanne repeated as her eyes frantically
glided over the numbers that coated the thick walls.

"Baby, you have to calm down," Shyanne heard Darrien
advise. She heard him, but she was not listening. They had only
been married for three days and were already facing more trauma.

"Dang it! We're on the wrong floor! We've got to get back
on the elevator." Shyanne was annoyed at this point. "Come on!
Come on! Come on!" She exclaimed with fury as she pressed the
cold "up" button on the wall next to the elevator.

"Baby," Darrien said.

"What?" Shyanne snapped and immediately regretted it.
The piercing expression on his face and his furrowed brow
brought Shyanne back to reality.

"I'm sorry, honey," Shyanne reasoned in a calmer tone.
"I'm just nervous."

"I know, but you have to calm down," Darrien expressed as he lovingly caressed her left cheek. "Look, the elevator is here."

Shyanne's handsome husband held the elevator door as she walked in. Although they were only going up one level, it felt like twenty. Shyanne's heart was beating on overtime. She nervously toyed with her ~~engagement and~~ wedding rings as the door opened.

Darrien and Shyanne swiftly got off the elevator searching for room 7260. The pair turned right and saw a waiting room hosting a sea of familiar faces. Shyanne could barely hear the "Hi, Pastor" and "Hey, First Lady" comments over the click-clacking sounds of her heels colliding with the floor's tile. She was not trying to be rude or ignore the people, she was just on a quest to find 7260.

"There's 7250, we have to turn left," Darrien said as he grabbed her hand and gently pulled her in the right direction.

7252.

It was a good thing Darrien was holding Shyanne up because with each step she took, her Berkshire covered legs grew weaker and weaker.

7254.

Shyanne's stomach began doing somersaults inside her skin as she saw a physician cover some unknown person's face with a blanket.

7254.

This was the second hospital Shyanne had been to just days apart. She could not believe this was her life.

7258.

Oh God, oh God, Shyanne thought to herself. It felt as if Darrien had to drag her into 7260.

"Jesus," Shyanne cried just above a whisper.

Darrien maneuvered behind Shyanne as she stood at the door. He began to rub her arms and shoulders. He was whispering something, but Shyanne could not hear him. The sight before her had robbed her of her other four senses. She cried and looked on silently as her parents, Skylar, Steven, Jr., Kyra, and Lisa surrounded her sister in a cocoon of love.

As Shyanne walked over to the bed, the sound of her heels caused them all to turn around and acknowledge her presence.

"Oh God," Lady Eva struggled to get up and greet her with a hug.

"Hi, Ma," Shyanne said and cried with her mother. Bishop Lawson just sat in his chair looking at Selena—it was like he was in a trance.

"I'm sorry," Shyanne said, "I rushed all the way up here after service."

"I was wondering why you still had on your church clothes," Lady Eva said, while giving Shyanne the once over. "You look beautiful," she added, as she used her fingers to brush Shyanne's hair strands into their rightful place.

"I'm sorry. I snatched my hat off in the car. I'm sure my head looks a mess."

"Well, hi, strangers," Kyra interjected, greeting Shyanne and Darrien with a hug. Lisa followed suit. "Shyanne, I'm glad you left your hat today; and Pastor, Cole is in the waiting room."

Kyra was throwing major daggers towards the Roberts. She had not forgotten how Selena told her Shyanne had hung up in her face earlier that day.

"I saw him on the way in. I'm actually going to stay in here and stand by my wife's side if that's ok with you, Sis. Kyra," Darrien said then pulled Shyanne close and kissed her on the cheek as he glared at Kyra.

"Ok, you two," Shyanne said in an attempt to cut the tension in the room. "Mom?"

Lady Eva's red eyes looked up at Shyanne, glossy. She was right by Selena's side, rubbing her hand. For the first time in a long time, Shyanne saw the true, outstanding beauty in her mother. She was vulnerable. Even in her loungewear, she looked beautiful. Her mother and father were everything she aspired for her and Darrien to become. Although Shyanne had not seen it before, her mother taught her everything she needed to know about becoming a wife, and a pastor's wife.

"Yes?"

"I called my attorney on the way over here. They are getting detectives involved. Whoever did this will not get away with doing this to Lena!" Shyanne said as she began to cry again.

"All I can tell you is that it was a female," Kyra offered.

"Wait, how do you know that?" Shyanne said.

"After you hung up on her earlier, Selena called me to talk and I was on the phone when the attack happened. I had Cole to call the police, so I could stay on the line and listen in case the person revealed who they were."

"Did they?" Bishop Lawson finally spoke.

"No, the only thing the person said was that Selena made them do it and something about a baby, and then I heard sirens."

Everyone got quiet and their eyes drifted to the hospital bed that was holding their friend, their sister, their daughter – Selena. She was hooked up to several machines, a tube hung from her mouth to assist her with breathing, and an IV pumped nutrients in liquid form into her veins. Selena's chest moved up and down as she laid there unresponsive. Her arms were tied to the bed to prevent her from snatching the tube from her throat in case she woke up.

Kyra, Lisa, and Selena were the closest people to Shyanne besides Darrien. Kyra, Lisa, and Selena were her circle – her sisters. Well, Lisa and Kyra figuratively; but Selena was her blood. They all grew up together, straight up church girls.

Shyanne's heart was filled with so much regret. She wished she could have stayed in Chicago. Or maybe she could have moved her sister to Carbondale? She wished she would have made time for her sister that morning instead of being so preoccupied with her new position. Selena was never too preoccupied for her sister. She put everything to the side to make Shyanne's dreams become reality.

Shyanne looked at Kyra. She knew Kyra loved her, but she had a feeling she, too, blamed Shyanne for the state Selena was in. Kyra was her ace. She was so filled with wisdom and love. She was a preacher's wife, but she was able to not let the church world consume her. She was a great wife to Cole and an awesome friend. As she eyed Kyra, she noticed she had gained a few pounds. *See, those church mothers love to fatten up the Pastor and First Lady!* Shyanne thought to herself. She made a mental note to stay in the gym.

Then there was crazy Lisa. She was the most adventurous of the four friends. Shyanne was the first person Lisa called when she lost her virginity at eighteen. Lisa rocked to the beat of her own drum, and was not concerned with anyone else's. The truth was, Lisa was deeply hurt by her father's passing and was acting out. Partying and sexing was not the core of who Lisa really was, but Shyanne just prayed for her friend.

Shyanne looked at her parents, Skylar, Steven, Jr., Lisa, Kyra, Darrien, and then at poor Selena. Shyanne could not believe her life at this moment. Just one week ago, she got engaged; days after her engagement, her father in love has a stroke; two days later, she wed; now this. Shyanne Janelle Lawson-Roberts was living in a state of shock.

Shyanne was determined to find out who had done this to her sister. The fact that Kyra heard the person say, "You made me do this" let Shyanne know it was someone Selena knew. She and her attorneys would get to the bottom of it and soon.

"Oh, God!" Shyanne exclaimed as an Earth-shattering sound interrupted her thoughts. One, single note sang by the heart monitor sent Shyanne crashing to her knees waiting in tears.

Sheridan S. Davis

Sheridan S. Davis is a 27-year-old Chicago native. She was born into a sanging, preaching, entertaining family, thus she follows the same trend. Her mother is recording artist, Pastor Trina Davis, and her father is Apostle, Prophet Joseph E. Davis (of Word for the World Ministries, International). Therefore, it was no surprise that Sheridan and her siblings grew up singing and entertaining.

She's done her fair share of acting in theater and music theater; now, she can add writer and director to her growing list of accomplishments, as she wrote and directed her first stage play, "Pretty for A Dark-Skin Girl," in May of 2016.

Sheridan has been releasing and writing books since May of 2014. This list includes: "Saved Sex," "Pretty for a Dark-Skin Girl," "I'm Nobody's Ruth," and "Church Girls". The last two have been released under her publishing company, Chocolate Chip & Co.

Sheridan S. Davis has been a licensed minister for 3 years and is well on her way to becoming a mogul, taking the world by storm one person at a time.

Sheridan S. Davis

CPSIA information can be obtained
at www.ICGtesting.com
Printed in the USA
LVHW072301171019
634536LV00001B/2/P

* 9 7 8 1 7 2 7 2 0 8 5 5 9 *